Sorry I Worried You

Winner of the

Flannery O'Connor Award

for Short Fiction

Sorry I Worried You

STORIES BY *Gary Fincke*

The University of Georgia Press | Athens and London

Published by the University of Georgia Press

Athens, Georgia 30602

© 2004 by Gary Fincke

All rights reserved

Printed and bound by Edwards Brothers

The paper in this book meets the guidelines

for permanence and durability of the

Committee on Production Guidelines

for Book Longevity of the Council on

Library Resources.

Printed in the United States of America

08 07 06 05 04 C 5 4 3 2 1

Library of Congress Cataloging-in-Publication Data

Fincke, Gary.

Sorry I worried you : stories / by Gary Fincke.

     p. cm. — (The Flannery O'Connor Award for

Short Fiction)

ISBN 0-8203-2656-9 (alk. paper)

1. United States—Social life and customs—Fiction.

2. Working class—Fiction. I. Title. II. Series.

PS3556.I457S67 2004

813'.54—dc22   2004007413

British Library Cataloging-in-Publication Data

available

Contents

The Lightning Tongues 1

Sorry I Worried You   16

Cargo   38

The History of Staying Awake 53

Piecework   68

The Serial Plagiarist   85

Wire's Wire, until It's a Body   101

Rip His Head Off   121

Book Owner   150

Pharisees   165

The Armstrong View   186

Gatsby, Tender, Paradise   202

Acknowledgments   217

Sorry I Worried You

The Lightning Tongues

One of the pleasures of working day shift at the newsstand at the mall is popping open the paper bundles, arranging them by local, state, and national, and then taking one of each into the back room to keep me company through a large coffee and a Long-John from Donut Queen.

I don't mind not getting paid for the first fifteen minutes, but the second fifteen are on the clock. And though it isn't, I'll admit, a fringe benefit anybody I know would be pleased to have, the truth is I would read through the whole half hour for free, saving the local paper until last. Which was why I didn't find out, until five minutes before I had to unlock, that Stacey Long, who worked at the pet store next to the newsstand, had left for lunch yesterday at 12:30 and hadn't been seen since then.

I'd eaten lunch with her more than a few times, even when she was still married. By then she was happy to have me sit across from her at Arby's or Burger King because Wade, her husband, though she'd moved out, let it be known she still belonged to him and he wasn't about to truck with her shacking up behind his back.

"It might as well be you he imagines, Danny," she told me. "He knows who you are. He remembers you from high school."

I didn't think my having been a linebacker was any protection to her. I'd added thirty pounds of unhelpful fat in the ten years since I'd worn a helmet, and I'd never even been in a shoving match around a pileup. But if it made a skinny loudmouth like Wade Long keep his place, I was pleased to help, meanwhile trying to believe something real for him to fret about would sometime or another arise.

I stopped reading and looked at the picture her mother must have given the reporter because I didn't remember her hair long like that since she was married to Wade. He must have had a hundred pictures of her looking like she did in the here-and-now instead of five years ago, but I admitted to myself there were more reasons than guilt for not giving up such a photo. And when I saw it was 9:02, that I was already late with opening, there was Wade Long himself fidgeting at the door.

It was daylight. I equated sunshine with safety. A well-lit place like the mall made me relax. I unlocked the door as if Wade were there to buy lottery tickets or a cigar or a sack of candy bars. "Don't this beat it," Wade said.

"You tell me, Wade."

"You ain't taken a mind to bein' one of them search party faggots?"

"I don't know anything about a search party, Wade. I have a job right here for the next eight hours."

"You don't have that much to do. I seen how you work your own damn self right over to where them puppies yammer all the damn day."

"You're mistaking lunch for sex, Wade."

Wade bounced from one foot to the other, tapping the set of keys in his right hand against the door frame. "I got to give it to you getting to the point, Danny. That's why I'm here—clear the air and all."

"The air here is clear, Wade."

"She could have herself sitting in a motel somewhere watching the television and laughing at Wade Long getting hassled by the police. They talking about my involvement, and there ain't nothing happened far as I can make out."

"The paper says her car's still out in the lot."

"With all that yellow tape and shit around it like the front seat was covered with blood. With the police standing around looking at me like I had her stuffed up my shirt." A group of old people walked by, finishing the walking trail they followed each morning before the stores opened. Wade looked them up and down as if he were checking for a plainclothesman.

"Listen up, Danny," Wade said. "Guilty men don't come back. That's mythology made up by cops. You see me standing here. You see proof."

"The ex post facto alibi."

"Yeah," Wade said. "Whatever. You can see I'm investigating on my own. Looking for the weak links is looking out for my own self in this sorry mess where the bullseye's on my back."

"I'll tell everybody you're looking for clues," I said.

Wade settled down and smiled. "There you go," he said, "though she fucked with me, I'll admit to thinking. She done me wrong."

"You don't kill somebody for being unfaithful."

"You best be careful making such judgments. I didn't say nothing about her fucking another man. I took care of her needs. I did right by her. It was her all the time being smart."

"It's not something that comes and goes like lust."

"You weren't so smart in school. I remember you, Danny. You just kicked ass on the football field and waited for the girls to think that was some kind of foreplay. You went in the navy like any hick jackass. You didn't go to any college, even for football."

In the front of the pet store, under glass, are toads and lizards you can waken with a quarter, dropping crickets or flies to their lightning tongues. I did it once and threw away two dollars in three minutes. It was like being drunk and feeding a one-song jukebox, listening to eternal heartbreak driving down the booze-sloshed two-lane to hell in a nasal twang. Stacey, a week ago, had sold a pair of hermit crabs to my sister's boy Dale. She'd given him 10 percent off for being under twelve, and before he showed me the crabs he described the last seconds in the life of the cricket his quarter had paid for.

When I left the mall for lunch, I walked by Stacey's car. It was like looking at a black hole, all of it dark with vacancy. I kept going, set on ending up at Hardee's at the end of the lot, but just like that, passing it, I started imagining one of those chalked outlines of her body in the driver's seat, set it upright, one foot on the brake, so maybe she could climb back into that shape, fitting it so exactly she could reclaim herself. And as soon as I turned my back to that car, I was sure she was dead.

On the television news at 6:00, the police said they'd had Wade Long in for questioning, but no arrest had been made. Their big news was a film clip from a security camera at the drive-through teller at the mall. Stacey's car was parked a couple of spots down from the window, and they'd watched the film until a woman showed up beside that car at 12:32.

"A man walks into the picture," the police chief explained. "It's fuzzy because the two of them aren't threats to the bank so far away, but he puts his hands on her all right, and they leave together in another car." The chief looked at the camera. "We think this is important evidence," he finished, and I had to agree that if you were a policeman looking to hang Wade Long for murder, you pay attention to the way the man holds the woman by the shoulders with both hands, how he turns her and leads her out of the picture. Blurry or not, you start to think "Wade and Stacey Long," and when a car turns past the camera ten seconds later, you figure the two people inside aren't going to lunch together.

"Could be anybody," Wade says to the same reporter as he leaves the police station. "You wouldn't recognize your own self in that movie." He's dressed exactly as he was at 9 A.M., the faded green T-shirt tucked into his jeans. I half expected him to start tapping his keys as he said, "I ain't done nothing to be ashamed of."

"The FBI has better equipment," the police chief comes back to announce to the camera. "We'll see who's the star of this movie."

Lottery tickets are a bigger draw at the newsstand than the newspapers and magazines. So is tobacco. The flavored kind people who read a lot of books put in pipes. Cherry, especially.

I kept track for a week once. Forty-eight of the fifty-four men who bought cherry tobacco were wearing ties. It tells you something about the ways the world divides itself, but there's nothing I can do with the things I've learned.

At 9:05 the next morning, a policeman arranged himself in the doorway like someone who was used to blocking the fastest way to open spaces. "You Danny Race?" he asked, and when I nodded as I slid my set of papers back into their racks, he added, "I expected so," and he kicked the stopper from under the door to swing it shut.

"You an acquaintance of both the Longs, Wade and Stacey?"

"You could say that."

"All right, I'm saying that. You close with them?"

"Not hardly."

"But you've been seen socially with Stacey?"

"Lunch. She works next door."

"Lunch."

"She was afraid of Wade, if that's what you need to know."

"Love hurts," the policeman said. "You remember that park ranger in Virginia, that guy who was hit by lightning seven times and lived?"

"The one who's in the *Guinness Book*?"

"Well, he's not going to make that record harder to beat. He went out and killed himself over lost love. The woman he wanted hauled ass on him. Don't make no kind of sense, does it? He should of known better." He looked up and down the newspapers as if he expected to see Stacey's disappearance on the front page of *USA Today* and the *New York Times*. "That's why I'm here, Danny. In my experience, a man does harm to the woman, not himself."

In the pet store, near the front counter where Stacey worked, is a glass cage containing an enormous iguana. "Can't sell something this big," Stacey explained once. "Nobody wants something that doesn't recognize them as someone it depends on, not for two thousand dollars they don't."

I looked at the iguana every time I walked by the store, remem-

bering the one I had owned, how it had always climbed up and toward heat—lamps, window shades, bookcases. When it had turned
lethargic and refused to eat, I had fed it baby food on the advice of
the pet-store manager. For a while, that did the trick—the iguana
gobbled jar after jar of pureed vegetables, and then its skin had gone
slack, and it seemed suddenly unable to move anywhere except
slowly across level surfaces.

"Who the hell told you that?" the veterinarian had asked when
I'd carried the iguana, two days before it died, into his office for a
miracle. The steady diet of baby food, he explained, had turned the
iguana's bones to mush.

I didn't hate the pet-store manager for his bad advice. I hated him
for being the last man Stacey Long had slept with before she'd been
killed. There was nothing about the man worth dying for.

At the end of my shift I made sure to walk in the pet store when
I saw he was on the floor. "You're Danny Race, am I right on that?"
he said when I placed myself in front of him beside the huge
iguana's cage.

"I'm a friend of Stacey's."

"Aren't we all."

I knew the manager's name was Chet Gable, but he'd have to
introduce himself without my prompting. Already I felt stupid and
lost, as if I'd walked miles since I'd left the newsstand. What did I
think, that the man, ten years older than me, small and drab with a
voice to match, could be possessive enough to threaten anyone? The
police, I was certain, had eliminated him as a suspect as rapidly as
they had erased me. I wished I had never done more than listen to
his outline of the baby food treatment, when nothing about his voice
or his appearance or the words he chose made any difference to me.

"Police talk to you about all this?" I said.

The manager tapped on the glass to get the iguana's attention. "No business of yours," he said.

"Right. None."

He slapped his palm on the glass, and the iguana's head swiveled so fast I took a step back. "You shouldn't come over here all full of piss and vinegar," he said. "Your football days are old news. I'm the one ought to be casing you and your sorrow for never getting what you wanted from that poor girl."

The iguana turned and settled. "You had one of these die on you, didn't you?" the manager said. He took his hands off the glass and stared at me. "Listen," he said, "did you read about those poor bastards got killed on that elevator that dropped twenty-one floors?"

"Yeah," I said, despite myself. Six passengers. The story had made every paper we stocked.

"They had a chance to live, you know. Any one of them if he had jumped up," he said, "at exactly the right moment, would've been OK. Those other guys would have been smashed, and he would've walked out of there like Jesus Christ his own self."

"There's simple math that says you're wrong," I said, though I wouldn't have been able to come up with the figures if he asked me.

"You saying you wouldn't try to jump?"

"I'm saying it's hopeless once that elevator gets going."

"A man's got to take what's available. He can't let himself turn to shit. That's a sorry thing to do with the one chance he's got."

He stared at me as if he'd just finished a book on mind control, but he didn't have to be silly about it. I'd already decided to drive to Wade Long's and shoot him before the police arrested him. The situation was as simple as anything else that had ever happened to me. I was sure of that because otherwise I would have gotten stuck long ago.

Thirteen days it took, but somebody rooting through trash dumped off a back road eight miles from the mall found a body. "Most likely the missing woman," the police said, though they had to admit they didn't know for sure, and they were lucky to have any dead body at all.

It was Stacey all right, though it took a day to confirm it through her teeth and whatever else they use in these cases. I waited another day. I gave all the gawkers their chance to drive by and get waved along by the police, the chief saying he would get to Wade Long, who knew enough not to run, if a few more things fell into place.

I parked my car in the only place Wade could have pulled off the road. I imagined how it would be to tug a blanket-wrapped body out of my trunk and managed the job in my head until I gave the body the identity of somebody I knew. And then, regardless, I got stuck in my thinking.

What I had to do, because I'd come to believe I was obligated to do nobody harm on the chance they had a decency disguised by obnoxious behavior, was convince myself Wade Long was the sorriest shithead ever born, because if someone like me could kill a woman I'd lived with, there was no hope for the world. But as soon as I stepped over the guardrail and skidded down the hillside, I knew that fifty feet from the highway the world belonged to the brutal and the instinctive who drift us darkly toward the recklessness in ourselves.

Where the ground went level again, it ran so bare and narrow it might have been the towpath for a canal invisible behind the brush. It was a flash-flood ravine, the kind of crevice that turns, after a spare tire or two, into a landfill, and I followed the footholds for those who scavenged this illegal dump, cleaning up after the slingers of broken televisions and lawnmowers, mattresses and bedsprings, a sort of filter for trash, for the anger that snaps a spine or seals shut a throat. From where I stood, it could have been a sluiceway to the ocean, the next heavy rain sweeping away a month of filth.

Somewhere down in the gully I expected the yellow tape of crime scenes, but aside from the skunk cabbage and itchweed and three kinds of ferns being trampled, the site looked like anyplace else where sumac and locust would try to start a forest as soon as nobody showed up for a couple of weeks. I tried to imagine the body of Stacey Long lying here, the blanket she'd been wrapped in undone, but all I could see were people alive and well and unmindful of what they were trampling underfoot as they drank beer and listened to music on battery-driven boom boxes while they picked through litter.

There's a college in the next town over from the mall. Even if you don't sell cherry tobacco to the professors, you know it's there just by sitting in the bars. A mile outside of town and the customers are all locals, men like Wade and me drinking cheap drafts, or if we're feeling poorly, using those drafts to chase whiskey and make us think we're about to get lucky with some woman in jeans who's not carrying the extra pounds of greasy food and all-day television.

In town, after 9:00, kids in designer clothes with trendy haircuts start filling up the three bars. It's time to move on or get depressed, watching twenty-year-olds from another state acting like they know something Mommy and Daddy and Professor Pipesmoker haven't told them.

But those girls make you want to sign up for a couple of classes. I've seen Wade tail-chasing a few times, and he looks so pathetic I've kept my mouth shut until I can escape to where every woman in the bar lives within five miles of its front door. None of those girls from New Jersey or Maryland read the local papers. They don't know how easy a man like Wade can be set off to violence. Last week they held a rally up there on their big lawn—five hundred of those girls holding candles and chanting "Take back the night." It makes me wonder which of those beauties will end up bagged in a gully because she thinks the world's changing.

I'd seen Stacey the morning of the day she disappeared. I'd unlocked the newsstand door, and she was setting out the toads and lizards. "If I give you ten dollars," I said, "could I set all the crickets free?"

Stacey smiled. "Danny," she said, "something else will just eat them."

"Not right away. Not with kids and their mothers watching."

"What would these hungry guys do then? You'd have to set them free, too."

"One thing leads to another."

"Always, Danny," she said, looking past me toward the mall entrance. When I glanced back, I saw a man in a muted, pin-striped suit. He turned toward the window of the card shop and tucked a few strands of his silver hair back into place. "Yours or mine?" Stacey asked, and when the man studied himself a second time, I said, "I'll give him quarters for change," thinking that if she stood beside the toads and lizards the man in the suit would ask for a roll of quarters to empty that box of crickets.

Under the counter, inside a copy of the *Harrisburg Patriot* the owner updated every Friday, was a handgun he kept. When I left work at

5:30, I slid it into the inside pocket of my blazer. It felt so heavy in my pocket that I thought the jacket was hanging lopsided, that Wade would notice and then throw himself on me or run, either choice guaranteeing no harm to himself. Each time I had imagined myself shooting Wade, he didn't move when I aimed the gun. He stood his ground and said, "Fuck you."

Wade had a double-wide set back on three acres of reclaimed strip mine. I'd dropped Stacey off one day a month back when her car wouldn't start after work, and I'd asked her about the fenced-in stretch above their trailer. "Wade says it's a surprise," she'd said. "But what else could it be but horses?"

I remembered that now because Wade was between the trailer and the nearest fence, and he didn't have horses behind it. "Lookit who come to sightsee," he said as I walked toward him, stopping a few steps away to get my breath settled from the uphill climb. "I'm raising llamas," Wade said. "I'm tired of doing ordinary shit."

I looked at the animals and at once thought I was in a zoo. They were so foreign that they made everything else seem artificial as well. When the police arrived, they'd think they were in some sort of theme park, that there were other exotic animals that might lunge out of the woods to do them harm. Already, I knew it was a mistake to let Wade talk, even a sentence or two. It would have been easier, I realized, to have run him down with my car.

"They're something, Wade," I said. "I'll give you that."

"Think I'm stupid?" Wade said. "You selling Pick-Seven tickets to suckers and thinking you're smarter than everybody else in the world. They're just customers, fella. They don't make you a genius."

"It wouldn't matter if I didn't work there," I said. "I'd rightly agree to that."

Dark clouds were scudding up from behind the patch of pines the coal company had planted before they packed up and left twenty years ago. I needed to get this done before rain gave me a reason to say "another time."

"What matters out here, Danny?" Wade said. "You got yourself some work needs doing?"

"Delivery boy, maybe. I'm not exactly sure."

"You the pizza guy for the do-gooders?"

I wanted to stop talking. This was what justice meant. What you were willing to do. "I'm not a support group," I said. "This isn't the AA for despair." And I understood that if I pulled out the gun, Wade would shoot me with it.

The wind sprayed a mist across the hillside. I had to choose which foolishness I could live with. "You know anything about llamas?" Wade said. He blinked as if the rain was falling harder where he stood, ten feet from me. He folded his hands together and cracked his knuckles.

"No," I said.

"Danny, what the hell do you know about anything?"

I looked back at the stand of pines that was fading into the weather's early twilight and said, "Moss grows on the north side of trees."

Wade snorted and shoved his hands into his jeans pockets. "Bullshit it does. Moss grows where it's dampest—north, south, east, west—all around the damn compass. You Boy Scouts—next you'll be telling me you can't rip the tag off your mattress."

Suddenly he yanked his hands up, waved them at the llamas, and said, "Danny, you haven't the balls," so exactly right, I could say nothing. One llama looked our way, and the other five all turned and stared, though it seemed they weren't registering the two of us. "You need passion, Danny," Wade said, "and let me tell you, the little dashboard light is beaming so bright anybody riding with you knows there's a godawful need for refueling."

"But I can fill up again and keep going, Wade. I'm free to get somewhere else."

"You got the wish-I-didn't-have-my-freedom blues. You should have stayed in the navy and let somebody decide everything for you. This way you know you're hopeless—the other way you could pretend things would be different if you ever got yourself back on land."

The rain settled into steady. I only owned one other sport coat besides the blazer that was getting soaked. Wade could toss his T-shirt on the floor of his double-wide and put it back on tomorrow morning. "What happens to the llamas if the FBI says they recognize you?" I said.

"I tie them out back of the pet store. I lay the guilt for their demise on that prick who was pumping Stacey. I know for a fact I don't have to leave any by the magazine stand, though honest-to-God, Danny, I wish it was you fucking her cause I don't rightly know what's in that manager made a woman spread her legs."

"I can't say I know either, Wade," I said, and then both of us laughed.

"You want to show me your popgun?" Wade said.

"No."

Wade fixed my eyes with his. "That's good. You keep some things to yourself in this world."

I nodded, but the handgun seemed as ludicrous as a battery-powered dildo. The owner of the newsstand couldn't possibly expect to be robbed. Who would risk himself on the store least likely to have a decent take in the register? And then Wade turned and ran at the fence, yelling, "Stop staring, you stupid fucks," the llamas bolting silently until they reached the opposite fence where they turned sideways and looked back at Wade as if they could feed and water themselves every day until he'd served his sentence.

The next day the FBI-enhanced pictures made the police think the district attorney could convince a jury Wade and Stacey Long were responsible for the blurry images moving between cars. I asked for night shift. It would keep me busy until 10:00. By that time I could pretend I've been somewhere and I'm coming home to watch the news and fall asleep like people who aren't angry every minute they're not busy with something. Wade hasn't been in the papers since he was arrested and couldn't make bail. He'll have to wait until his trial to get quoted again about the injustices of circumstantial evidence.

What I've learned is the women who work late all park together under two lights. Each night I come out and see their dozen cars clustered and the rest, twenty or more, scattered all the way to the various darknesses in the mall lot.

I've started parking among the women. It spooks them a little to see a man jiggling a key at a lock when they come out in pairs or groups of three. What do they think when they see me there? That I'm parked among them for my own protection? That I'm a boyfriend or a husband of one of the women in a different group?

Do they slide their keys between their fingers like they've been taught in self-defense class? Do some of them reach into their purses for cans of Mace or electric prods? Or do they recognize me as that guy who sold them a lottery ticket a few days back, somebody so familiar he couldn't possibly be dangerous?

Sorry I Worried You

"Did you know," Dr. Parrish asked, "that there are birds who learned to open milk cartons? They pecked and lifted until they could get at the cream at the top."

"There hasn't been cream on the top of milk since I was kid," Ben said.

"Exactly. This was way back. Before they stopped using those foil caps and started in with those impossible to open spouts. OK, now, bend over for me."

She'd started these exams the year Ben Nowak had turned fifty. For three years now, Ben had told himself if he had known what was coming, he would have changed doctors, but she'd announced it nonchalantly at the end of his annual exam, pulling on a latex glove and shoving herself inside him. Worse, Lori Rousch, who was married to his friend Jerry, had become the receptionist that same year, and she was someone, Ben was sure, who would thumb through files when things slowed down in the office.

Two years ago, the second time Dr. Parrish had examined him, he'd shriveled in the air conditioning and his nervousness. "Good," she'd said, "nice and small," and he'd felt the mix of relief and humiliation that comes, he thought, from being rescued.

Later, Ben had wondered what Dr. Parrish had thought as he leaned over the table, his ass bared, his genitals hanging between his spread legs. She'd been his doctor for fifteen years; she was divorced and available, seven years younger than he was, attractive enough that he'd stared at her body, imagining it naked, while she pressed a stethoscope to his chest.

"Unhhh," he breathed now, astonished at how this exam always rushed the air out of him. And when she hesitated, not saying "Good" as she had repeated the three previous years, he froze, gripping the edges of the padded table.

"OK," she said, turning away to discard the glove, but the extra five seconds made him say "Really?" as he tugged his pants up.

"You're a little larger," she said. "That happens." Ben waited. "We'll see what the lab says. It's probably just another inevitable change."

"Like death," he said, but she didn't change her expression.

"Come on, Ben. Let's not be melodramatic. Usually it just means you'll be getting up in the middle of the night from now on."

"Hey there, Ben," he heard Lori say as he walked by, and when he gave her a short-armed wave instead of stopping to talk, he knew she would be into his file before the afternoon was over.

When Ben walked into work at the bookstore, his assistant manager Shelly was pacing and crying in the back room. He looked at Erin, a part-timer, who was sitting on a crate and repeating encouragements like a coach. "It's only stuff," she kept saying. "Nobody's hurt."

"What?" Ben finally asked after Shelly passed a second time without slowing down.

"Shelly got ripped off."

He thought of what he kept in the back room. A spare shirt, a toothbrush, magazines he brought back from the shelves and forgot to replace. "What was stolen?" he said.

"Three pairs of shoes, my Walkman, and twenty-four CDs," Shelly screamed.

Erin shrugged. "Inventory," she said. "It's our job."

Kyle, thirty hours a week like Erin, stuck his head in the back door. "Don't sweat the CDs," he said.

Shelly shut up and looked at him. "You replacing them for me?" she asked, as if something miraculous might occur in the back room of Read-A-Lot.

"Don't have to," he said, sweeping an arm toward the open door.

They all tramped into the alley that led to Rush Street. There was a trail of CDs all the way to the stoplight. Celine Dion. Jessica Simpson. Whoever had stolen Shelly's stuff had pitched the CDs. The cases were open, and a couple of the CDs were lying loose — Mandy Moore. Dream. Greatest Television Love Themes. Kyle began to laugh. "The thief must have said, 'Fuck this shit' and tossed them all away."

"How come nobody else had anything stolen?" Shelly asked.

"We don't have anything to steal," Kyle said.

"It's somebody who works here. It has to be."

"Where's that come from?" Ben said.

She glanced at the others. "They know." She reset the two CDs that had popped loose from their cases. "Go ahead, say it."

"OK," Kyle said. "It's a joke."

"I don't get it," Ben said.

"It's a setup to make fun of my CDs, OK?"

A pigeon settled onto Jessica Simpson and pecked at the cover. "For sure," Kyle said, "that bird has no taste."

Ben smiled. "Did you know," he said, "there were birds once that figured out how to open the foil caps on bottles of milk to get at the cream."

"Cream?" Shelly said. "That sounds gross."

"Where were the bottles?" Kyle said, and Ben knew his story was in trouble.

"The milkman used to leave them by the front door. It was before milk was homogenized, and the cream rose to the top."

He held the door open for Shelly, who was keeping both hands on her CDs. Shelly looked at him. "If you're old enough to remember the milkman bringing milk with cream on the top, you're older than I thought." She was in her late twenties, he thought, half his age. He needed to shut up about the 1950s. He had color in his hair; he had a flat stomach; concentrate your stories in the 60s, he said to himself; keep yourself under fifty years old.

After work he drove to Jerry Rousch's house. Friday was dump-beer night at Jerry's, when three or four guys from the neighborhood sat in Jerry's clubhouse, what he'd made out of the top half of his garage—a shrine, even from 150 miles away, to Pittsburgh sports. Jerry worked at the landfill, the last one within fifty miles. Though Jerry didn't talk about it, Ben had heard the landfill had less than ten years to go before it topped out and was closed, and Jerry, sensing the end of opportunity perhaps, had started, a year ago, to cart home cases of date-expired beer instead of covering them with dirt. By now his garage was full of beer. "Everything has an expiration date," Jerry had explained when Ben had remarked on the twenty-four cases of Genesee Cream Ale stacked in Jerry's garage, "but that doesn't mean it's spoiled."

"Where's Clemente?" Bob Slaney asked now, holding his first beer and following the pictures of the 1960 Pirates to the end of the wall.

Ben waited. Slaney was new, somebody who'd lived down the street for three months now, long enough, finally, to get an invite from Rousch. He hadn't noticed, somehow, that Rousch's wall was all white. The Steelers, the Penguins, the Pirates—it was as if they were sitting there fifty years before, when race wasn't an issue if you decorated with sports.

Rousch walked along the wall tapping on the pictures one by one. "Vernon Law," he said. "Bob Friend, Elroy Face, Dick Groat—that was a team. I was a junior in high school when they beat the fucking Yankees. Hal Smith, Bill Mazeroski—they won that seventh game. Clemente didn't win that 60 Series. These guys did."

Slaney nodded like that explained it, but he lifted his eyes to the 71 Pirates, and he was old enough, Ben was certain, to remember that Clemente had been the MVP of that World Series.

Rousch opened another round of Blue Ribbon, but Ben was still nursing his first. "You on the wagon?"

Ben swallowed off the rest and took the bottle from Rousch. "I just got told my prostate got bigger."

Rousch laughed. "By Lori's boss? You enjoy it?"

"If you're suicidal, you might."

Rousch looked over at Slaney. "I know," he said, "Clemente's not there either. And Stargell's not up there with the 1979 champs. He got lucky once—he tanked the other playoffs he was in."

Slaney turned and looked toward Ben as if he was deciding whether to ever come back or whether, Ben suddenly thought, how big an asshole Ben was to come back to Rousch's nearly every Friday.

Rousch dropped back into his recliner. "You worry too much. I'm fifty-eight. I piss every two hours. Like a fucking clock."

Ben watched Slaney shift to the Penguins, where the lineup didn't have holes in it. "It's panic that kills," Rousch said. "You want to hear a story? There's this woman sitting inside her car in a parking lot holding both hands to the back of her head until people walking by start to notice."

Slaney turned away from the wall and picked up the beer Rousch had opened. "'I've been shot,' she said to those passersby. 'I'm holding my brains in with my hands.'" Rousch took a swig and winked. "Well," he went on, "the paramedics came, and what did they see? The canned bread dough she'd bought had exploded in her hot car, flattening against her head like a fat glob of brains."

Ben forced a smile, but when Slaney laughed out loud, Ben knew the hall-of-fame issue was moot with him. "You know what one of the paramedics told a reporter?" Rousch said, and when Ben and Slaney shrugged, he added, "'She could have saved John Kennedy she was pressing so hard.'"

Ben thought it over and decided pie-filling would be more apt for brains, the sweet ooze of crushed berries and cornstarch swelling up through the fingers, no matter how heavily she pressed until she knew, suddenly, she was still thinking, wondering what part of her was seeping down her hands and over her wrists to confuse her fear, running up her arms like long-term memory, leaving her in the present. What did that woman think, driving off, after she moved past the great relief of recovery? That her story would spread? That she was never alive until she bungled the exam of common sense and held her head as if she wasn't already as good as dead?

"Maybe you ought to cut Stargell and Clemente some slack. We're getting too old to hold grudges."

"That's exactly why we do," Rousch said. "You're what—fifty-three years old? You're whoever the fuck you're ever going to be."

"I can't think like that."

"You'd have to blow your brains out not to think like that."

When the third Blue Ribbons were passed around, nobody else showing up on this first night for high school football, Slaney started reading the label as if it were covered with all the statistics from the Pirates' current miserable season. Ben watched for a moment, deciding that Slaney was one of those men who toyed with his third beer and then held his fourth for an hour while the rest of the room got drunk. He imagined Slaney telling stories at work about his crazy night at the all-white clubhouse, how trashed he'd been hanging with a crowd of new friends from the neighborhood.

Ben could see that Rousch noticed too, but for now he acted as if he was giving Slaney the benefit of the doubt. "I was looking for the expiration date on here," Slaney suddenly said, but he didn't put the bottle to his lips.

"It's there, all right," Rousch said, and then he bunched up his shirt in one hand and tugged it. "You'd be surprised what gets dumped. Shirts, for Christ's sake. You're there at the right time, and you can live off what's thrown away."

"Unless you worry about being in style," Ben said, and when Slaney laughed, looking at his bottle again, Ben started to hate him.

Rousch nodded and smoothed his shirt back down. "Dry Beer. Ice Beer. You dig up a dump, and you'll see all the beer fads layered right down to Hop 'n' Gator."

"What?" Slaney said, giggling, and Rousch, Ben happily observed, looked like he'd made up his mind about Bob Slaney. "It was Iron City's fag beer. A disgrace to Pittsburgh. It tasted like lime juice somebody pissed in. You see any regular beer downstairs? You see any Bud or Coors or Miller? No way they're down there because that's what gets sold. Down there is a museum for failure. All the fucking beers nobody gives a damn about."

Slaney backed up and reached behind him as if he was feeling for the absent Clemente picture. "So you can tell what sells by looking for what isn't there?" he said.

Rousch snorted and drained his Blue Ribbon, and Ben, showing solidarity, let half a bottle drain down his throat to keep up. "You ever get a shipment of CDs?" Ben asked.

"They don't expire; they just suck or don't suck."

"This girl at work, everybody was making fun of her CDs. Jessica Simpson. Mandy Moore. They were all by girls."

Slaney laughed. "Somebody ought to talk to that girl," he said, looking back at the wall as Rousch passed a fresh beer to Ben.

"What's so bad about those singers? Aren't they popular?"

"Listen to this guy," Slaney said. "What do you listen to?"

"Nothing."

"Everybody listens to music."

"No they don't."

Rousch looked at Slaney. "Fucking A they don't," he said.

Slaney shrugged. "Maybe you'll find two tickets to Britney Spears at the dump. Maybe some poor schmuck threw them in the garbage and pretended they were stolen so he didn't have to sit through that crap with his girlfriend."

When the phone rang the following afternoon, Lori Rousch on the line, Ben waited for reassurance. "Ben," she said, "Dr. Parrish wants to run through a second set of tests. The others are inconclusive, she says. She wants to make sure she's not alarming you for nothing or reassuring you when things aren't right."

Ben thought of the woman holding her brains in with her hands. It was all he could do to keep from cupping his groin. Instead, he got into his car and drove to the landfill. When he turned on the radio, he tried the pop-rock station, listening to four songs, none of which were by any of the girls he remembered from Shelly's CDs.

Ben parked, sitting in his car to watch Rousch lower the scoop and catch a bit of the mound of soil, carrying it and dumping it and smoothing it over the most recent garbage. There was some sort of regulation about the depth of that soil, Ben figured. He guessed it was easier to just run out an extra scoop when you got close rather than get down there and measure. After a while you'd have a feel for it, the depth.

Had anybody ever offered him money to level a layer over a body? Rousch had been doing this job for twenty years—surely he'd heard the subject raised. Stepping out of the car, Ben heard the tearing of metal and the crushing of glass, was surprised any sound reached him over the bulldozer's rumble. He walked a few steps closer, wishing, suddenly, that the bulldozer could do its work silently so he could hear the subtler sounds made by outdated things as they were buried.

Rousch was gesturing, and Ben stepped across soil that felt so uncertain he imagined breaking through the crust and sinking into whatever Rousch had covered last week. Rousch had found a baby a year ago. Newborn, dead—what extraordinary luck to spot something like that just before it was covered. Rousch had waded into the debris and lifted the body out and taken it to the police. The mother was found within hours. The police found out where the load had originated. They canvassed the neighborhood for recently pregnant women and discovered a woman with no baby, one who stonewalled until the man she lived with gave her up to shed a better light on himself. She'd given birth in a bathtub and allowed that child to drown. Twice during the investigation the newspaper had run a picture of Rousch over sidebars that suggested he was a hero.

"Thought I'd see what the hell you do for a paycheck," he said to Rousch.

"Christ," Rousch said, "for a second there I thought you were the fucking inspector."

Ben laughed. "What? You covering over some lousy pantsuits from K-Mart and keeping the Cheez-Whiz?"

Rousch grunted. "Cheez-Whiz doesn't expire," he said. "It lasts forever. Like plastic."

A truck pulled in, and Ben watched as Rousch waved it into position and it dumped what could have been his house and all its contents compacted into something that looked like the "found art" at the installation that had been erected at the nearby state university.

"Christ," Rousch said as the truck looped back toward the highway, "look at all that shit. Even crushing everything, this place has maybe five years left in it before it has to close." Ben nodded, wondering if Lori had relayed the details of his file, symptoms that would cause Rousch to grow sentimental with him. "What the hell," Rousch went on, "I'll be sixty-three by then, good and ready to retire. Let somebody else figure out where to dump all this shit. I'm doing the world a favor hauling some of it home with me."

Ben smiled and squinted at the compacted trash, trying to decipher where it had originated from the colors and textures. "I'm being watched," Rousch said. "Did I tell you that? One of these truckers must have brought it up that maybe everything isn't being buried up here."

"Really? Who would bother?"

"Exactly. It's not like I'm selling anything." Rousch leaned against the bulldozer and slid off the gloves he was wearing. "I need to empty my garage," he said. "You know what I mean?"

"What a waste," Ben said.

"It doesn't have to be. You can load up and take some home with you. You can share the bounty. I got thirty cases. I haven't touched anything here for a month now. I'm giving you first dibs before I ask some of the other guys or even that jerk-off Slaney."

"I don't know," Ben said.

"You're going to turn it down?"

"I'm cutting back. What would I do with ten cases?"

"Bullshit. You think you'll be arrested or something. You can drink it as long as it's in my garage."

"No, that's not it."

"Sure it is. Give me a better reason why you'd say *no*, and I won't change my mind about what a pussy you are."

"Your wife called me this morning. I need a second run-through on my prostate," Ben said, surprised when Rousch gave no sign of having heard this news before.

"So you're out here stalling around."

"I'm going in at noon when the Saturday hours end. She worked me in."

Rousch looked at him closely. "You think this might be the real thing?"

"I'm trying not to think."

"Forget about the beer then. I can get rid of it. It's not like I have a dead body in the garage."

"I didn't say *no* yet," Ben said. "Let me find out what's going on with this thing."

Rousch pulled his gloves back on as if he was satisfied. "OK."

Ben nodded toward the new shipment. "The only thing I ever buried was my favorite cap pistol when I was five years old. A Roy Rogers model. I covered it with sand beside some lake in Canada. I went back in the water. I thought I'd come out like a pirate and dig it up like treasure. The wind blew or something, or else I just lost track of where I was. Everything looked the same when I walked out."

"You have to landmark and fix a spot with something," Rousch said. "I could find anything I gave a damn about here. I know where things are if I wanted to dig."

"You cover beer this last month?"

"Nobody's brought any, and I sure as hell hope they don't."

"Sorry I'm late," Ben said, half sitting on the examination table in Dr. Parrish's office. The clock said 12:10. He'd been astonished that every patient had left already. The last time he'd had an appointment on the hour, he'd waited forty minutes before he'd been called.

"Putting things off doesn't help make them better."

"By ten minutes?" Ben said. Dr. Parrish frowned like a principal who heard that phrase twenty times a day. "You know where I was? I was watching your receptionist's husband bulldoze trash at the dump."

She brightened. "Jerry Rousch is a good man," she said. "I hope he's taking care of himself." She paused and then went on. "Listen, I have to take a closer look at you this time." She kept her eyes on him as he fidgeted. "A figure of speech," she said, and when his expression didn't change, she added, "I could just give you a doll like they used to give women patients in China."

"I don't get it," Ben said.

"Of course you don't. It's an old story we were told in medical school. It's the kind of inside joke doctors can pass around. But you still need to drop your pants."

Ben stood. He unbuckled his belt, listening to her. "The women would stay behind a curtain when the doctor came to see them. He would hand them a female doll for them to mark exactly where it hurt." He unzipped, tugged his pants and briefs down as he turned away from her. "Under an uplifted arm, for instance, they might charcoal a cross; low in the abdomen they might scratch an X."

"I don't have any pain," Ben said, leaning forward to grip the table. He grunted as he felt her enter him.

"Good," she said. "You're not getting a doll even if you were in agony. Even in those days men just laid there and took it."

Ben squirmed slightly. There was no reason to be self-conscious, he thought. She had to know how shyness shrunk men gone vulnerable in the groin. How many men, after all, had she asked to unbutton or unzip, turning discreetly away for a moment, giving them time to expose themselves with or without a med-school story?

And when she withdrew, stepping toward the sink, he watched her this time, thinking of how she knew when eternity began to form far out in the future's ocean. Instead of turning back immediately, she spoke as if he were glued to the wall in front of her. "The feet of those women behind the curtains were bound," she said. "They needed to wait for the doctor to come to them because they had difficulty even walking."

She pivoted, stripped her gloves, and he followed the intimate lines of her breasts and hips to the softness of himself, fixed until she turned, finally, in the last moment they were both deciding what was arriving. "Here," she said, "this is the book with the bird story in it. Read it for yourself, and I'll be back in a minute or two. The lab will take a second blood test. We need to make this call one way or the other."

Those birds, he read, learned to tug the cardboard tabs until the bottles opened, and then, when foil lids were the norm, poked holes and widened them until they could get at the cream. It wasn't the lids that stopped those birds; it was the advent of homogenized milk. The birds were lactose intolerant. And then, even though the birds learned to spot the color of the cap that said the milk was unstirred, home deliveries declined so severely they had to fly longer and longer to feed their habit.

Ben closed the book and listened for footsteps. His father, he remembered, had flown back to marbled meat, even after heart bypass; his mother, after stroke, had settled again and again on the salt of potato chips and pretzels. Christ, Ben thought, what was it, one out of ten men get prostate cancer? He had a lot of company coming if that was the case, and if his current lack of discomfort meant anything, he was going to be somebody who could say it was caught early. It wasn't even worth whining about. Every day he heard about something a hundred times worse.

"You'll have something to cry about when I'm through with you," his father used to say as he slapped a leather strap against his palm. Ben thought of him dead these twelve years, how he'd been eaten by pancreatic cancer, six weeks from diagnosis until death. He'd gotten something to cry about—a disease with a 3 percent cure rate. Dr. Parrish opened the door without him hearing her approach. "OK," she said, "let's do all the lab tests again."

"Monday afternoon," Lori said as Ben checked out after staring away from his blood filling the sample tube. "We'll have something for you by then." Ben nodded, and she smiled. "You helping Jerry get some of that damned beer out of our garage?"

"Maybe."

"You can drink as much of it as you want when you get good news."

Ben swept the waiting room with his eyes. He'd never seen it empty, and suddenly it seemed as if this was the way a doctor's office looked when you were seriously sick. That all of the ordinary coughing men and fever-ridden women kept appointments scheduled under *temporary inconvenience*. That once they'd filed out with prescriptions, the doors opened for *the shit out of luck*.

Ben drove to the bookstore, something he did so rarely on a Saturday he thought he could pass for a customer, testing whether Kyle or Shelly would bother to approach him and offer help in the pleasant voice that was supposed to signal they read books when they weren't trying to sell them. Instead, he let himself in the back door like always, walking in on Shelly swaying to whatever seeped through her headphones. "Oh," she said, yanking the earphones off. "Mr. Nowak. What are you doing here on a weekend?"

"Just passing by."

"I'm on break," she said, looking at her watch as if she knew exactly when she was expected back at the front desk.

"Your CDs still work," Ben said.

"Thank God."

"You take care," he said then, and he walked into the store, lifted a coffee-table book about the Pirates from the remainder bin, and walked straight past the empty front desk where one elderly woman stood tapping her Read-A-Lot discount card against a short stack of

Chicken Soup for . . . volumes. She stared at him as if she were memorizing his face for a lineup, but even if Kyle was sitting in the next-door pizza shop, Ben knew Shelly would reappear in a minute, and there was no one short of a customer with a dolly-load of hardbacks who could keep him in the store for another second.

Ben waited until Sunday night before he pulled into Rousch's driveway. "It's not Friday. You forget what day it is, or you here to load up?" Rousch asked, as the two of them stood outside the garage.

"I know what day it almost is—tomorrow, lab report day."

"Your problem's not a problem until they say it is," Rousch said.

"She's just protecting herself before she gives me the news. Beer or no beer, I already feel different."

Rousch shook his head. "You know Ellen Parrish does battered women sessions?"

"What?"

Rousch hesitated. "I thought everybody knew she claimed abuse by her husband as the reason for divorce."

"I don't have a set of ears in the office."

"It wasn't Lori who told me."

Ben thought about how Dr. Parrish would look as she examined him the next time. How her hands would feel knowing she'd used them to fend off her husband's fists. "Christ," Rousch said, "I think I'd just let myself swell up and die before I let a woman doctor feel me up like that. I don't care if Lori works there or not. I put my body in the hands of a man. It's Lori who tells me what to worry about with my health. If you had a wife, you'd have known this prostate thing was right around the next bend."

Rousch stared at Ben, moving a step closer as if he wanted to be certain of something before he went on. "You know what that fat fuck of a husband said when she accused him? 'I don't hit her. I keep my hands off her, and this is what I get for being a good guy.'"

"What did he say to her?"

"You're the one imagining things. Think about it."

"I don't know," Ben said. "Listen, I'll take the beer. You don't need to tell me."

Rousch looked at him, deciding. "Good," he said, opening the garage door.

Ben followed him inside. "So give me ten cases."

"I'll give you this," Rousch said. "You didn't wait to hear what that fat fuck asshole let loose from his mouth before you said *yes*."

"Just in time then."

"Yeah, just in time." Rousch didn't say anything for a moment. "Right," he said then. "Here's one more thing that fat fuck said to me, and then I'll drop it." He patted the top case of a stack of America's Best. "'God knows our thoughts,' he said, 'so what's the difference? Everybody thinks these things. It's just anger—she knows I'm thinking it, so what's wrong with saying it?' You tell me whether or not I thought I wanted to shoot that fucking bastard right then as he repeated that bullshit to me like a sermon."

"Her husband told you?"

"He was proud."

Ben gripped a case and slid it off the stack. "We're still thieves."

"No."

"That's what you think." Ben lifted the oversized Pittsburgh Pirates book off the front seat and handed it to Rousch. "Here's something in return at least."

Rousch grinned when he saw the title, and then he scanned the photographs on the cover. Ben remembered Clemente, Stargell,

Barry Bonds, Manny Sanguillen, Dock Ellis. There were more. Underneath those photos, right where Rousch was staring, was the subtitle: *The Minority Contribution to Pittsburgh Baseball*. "I stole it for you," Ben said.

"Sure you did," Rousch said. He tucked it under his arm. "You're not dying, Ben. You don't have to buy apologies for your sins."

"Lay it out for Slaney to look at if you let him back in the house."

Rousch snorted. "He was thinking it, wasn't he? If he was married to Ellen Parrish he'd be calling me something that ended in Ku Klux Klan."

Ben waited, but Rousch seemed distracted and awkward, getting ready for something he wanted to say but keeping both hands tucked under the book. "You take care," he finally said, "but don't you just be throwing those cases away as soon as you leave." He turned away and then pivoted back to face Ben. "You know what Slaney did the other night? He poured his third beer down the toilet when he went in to piss. I heard it. And then he came back out, took a swallow, and helped himself to a fourth like he wasn't so full of shit there wasn't room for free beer."

Though it was a night with no threat of rain, Ben parked in his garage, waited until the automatic light shut off, and then left the ten cases in his trunk and backseat as if not unloading them meant they weren't his yet.

The bookstore was closed on Monday. He had nothing to do in the morning but wait for the phone to ring. He listened to the radio for an hour and heard, finally, one of the names from Shelly's CDs—Mandy Moore. She sounded to Ben like Annette or Dodi Stevens, girl singers from his junior high school days who sounded so sweet it seemed tragic he'd never meet them. When the phone rang two songs later, he shut the radio off and counted to five before he picked up the receiver. "Good news," Lori chirped. "All the new tests are normal."

"What were the old tests?" he said at once.

"What do you mean?"

"The tests that told your boss to test again."

"I thought you'd be happy to hear this, Ben."

"I'm happier than I was."

"You want me to read you your PSA number? It's fine. You're fine, unless you think getting older is a disease."

"OK," Ben said, thinking, at once, *until the next time*. And then he walked to his car, deciding that even though it was daylight, he needed to toss the beer before he started thinking he owned it. He turned left two miles from home, followed the county road six miles, and when he saw the field of abandoned greenhouses, he remembered a maintenance road half a mile ahead that ended at the strip mine people used as an illegal dump.

He let the car slow. The greenhouses had been built to raise hydroponic tomatoes, a government grant funding the experiment of growing the plants in water. It had been nearly two years since the project folded, and yet, as he passed, Ben couldn't make out one pane of broken glass. This was more miraculous than escaping a medical scare, Ben thought, his reprieve already receding like delivered milk.

He found the dirt road and bumped along to the strip mine. He would finish one beer from each case, Ben decided, while he broke the other twenty-three bottles by flinging them into the rubble. That would be enough to tell Rousch, without lying, that he'd drunk his dump beer before he'd thrown away the cases. Rousch would stay away from Ben's house for a week or two so Ben wouldn't think his next visit was a search, and by the third week the absent cases would be plausible.

Ben downed the first America's Best, cringing at its watery bitterness, and lofted the empty toward a half-blackened refrigerator that hammered the top half of the bottle to shards. One by one he pitched the full bottles against the refrigerator, all of them bursting into glass chunks and froth. He broke the case down, folded the heavy cardboard over and laid it flat on the ground before he pried open a second case, twisted off a cap, and sat, finally, on a shelf of rock that had been polished by years of being used as a bench.

Settling down, Ben wondered if the police might come through here eventually, but it wasn't likely, he decided. On a Monday afternoon there wouldn't be partying teenagers or couples screwing in parked cars to harass.

For a minute he counted the pine trees scattered sparse on the sides of the hills that rose from the depression half-filled by refuse. Reclamation, Ben thought, giving up at fifty and beginning to drink his second beer. You plant a thousand trees and you can have a clear conscience, but those trees, so spread out on the ruined land, looked like they were sprouting from the skull of an enormous chemotherapy patient.

Rousch had told him, just before he pulled away with the beer, that the doctor's husband had called her a castrating bitch in public. "Which was the kindest thing he called her," Rousch had said. When Ben had asked how much more unkindly he'd spoken, Rousch had said, "Think of the difference between Negro and nigger."

Drinking and flinging bottles, Ben considered that difference. As little as an hour ago he'd wanted people he knew to fall sick or to fail at their work so he wouldn't be alone in despair. It didn't matter that he could no more say the words than he could lay his hands on Ellen Parrish or Shelly the dancing help. He'd become an asshole. Everything he kept to himself was so dreadful for so long it couldn't be spoken.

It didn't matter that he suspected everybody carried such a secret, that the only thing that prevented them from hating each other was silence. He wasn't excused because this was how the world managed, its days a collaboration based on a collective secret.

He drank off the second beer in three more swallows. He opened a third, managed one lengthy pull, and settled back to take his time with breakage, pitching the full bottles in a rhythm that would dictate the speed of his drinking each single to coincide with the last-destroyed of each twenty-three.

Halfway through the case he pushed himself up to choose a new target, noticing, instead, what looked like an infant half-buried under a pair of old tires. "Oh Christ," he thought, taking two steps toward it, his arms thrust out to the sides for balance, before he recognized it was a discarded doll.

It was just cans and bottles where he stood, and for a moment he didn't step back to where the case sat. That doll would fool anybody for a second, he decided, wondering if Rousch could have thought the opposite, that the baby he'd seen was a doll.

And then Ben decided there had to be at least one real infant in this makeshift landfill. That he could search among this trash while he drank beers four through ten. That if he found nothing today he could return the following day. There was a chance, if he searched daily, that the baby he found would be alive, that he could carry it to a hospital. Somebody would ask him what he was doing at the illegal dump, and he would say he'd been hiking for his health, something nearly true. Nobody would hold it against him that he might have just pitched half-used buckets of driveway sealer among the old tires and discarded batteries. They'd say it was serendipity, that he'd been guided by God.

He skidded out of the cans and bottles to open a beer from the fourth case, slowing his drinking now. He had nearly two hundred more bottles to toss. If some of them didn't break against the refrigerator, he would have to wade out, bring them back, and throw them again. He was going to sit there for two hours or more, enough that he should turn his car around now while the shifting and turning it took was still available to him.

Ben had seen pictures, once, of a spot on the earth taken from one foot, then ten feet, then one hundred feet, then a thousand, then ten thousand, then page after page of additional zeros to the distance until even the earth where that spot was became a spot, too, before it disappeared. By page five, he and his car full of beer would be gone. If the police didn't come before he finished, then he could keep this to himself. If they came he'd have to tell the whole story, and they'd have to listen.

Cargo

Just after 1 A.M., when I get home from another night of cleaning up after the basketball teams at our town's small college, my mother is sitting on the couch and holding a copy of *The Mother's Encyclopedia* in our darkened living room. "Did you know," she says, "that the year of the Bicentennial I was one-fourth the age of the country and you were one-eighth?"

"Yes."

"You never said."

"It doesn't have anything to do with us."

"I wish you would have."

"I'm sorry." That summer we drove into Pittsburgh for the fireworks at Point Park, slouched on blankets on the Allegheny side, and listened to an hour of John Philip Sousa played by a band that sat on board a tethered barge, and then the fireworks shot off right over our heads.

My mother was pleased. She'd gotten through a scare the winter before, chemotherapy and all the rest, and she'd come up clean in June, just about the time she'd called to tell me about the comeback of her favorite advertising icon, Speedy Alka-Seltzer. "I thought we were both goners," she said. "I thought this bicentennial birthday of mine was my last, and Speedy was lost on his way to the Philippines."

"I'm stumped," I admitted.

"Like Amelia Earhart. They put Speedy on a plane, and he disappeared somewhere out over the Pacific Ocean."

"His plane crashed?"

"No," she said, but I can't remember her explanation, only that she fed me Alka-Seltzer for every childhood ailment except skin diseases, and now she looks me up and down in the gloom as if she's assessing my health and says, "This year I'm 31.8 percent. It doesn't sound like anything."

I know where this is going because the cancer has returned. Or just as likely, it's a new cancer altogether that has settled into her bones. "Three-eighteen, Mom. Think of it as a batting average. You're a major leaguer."

"I don't think my average is going much higher. I think that's about it for my all-star days."

I do the quick math in my head and say, "I'm at two-oh-five, Mom. I'm just over the Mendoza line."

"The fellow who played for the Pirates. The little shortstop." I'm surprised, and she smiles. "Two hundred is the Mendoza line," she says. "It's a disgrace to fall any lower."

"I can't, Mom. I can only get higher."

"You be careful. It's harder for you than me to make three hundred. You'll need more than Alka-Seltzer."

"Seventy-five, Mom. I've done the math."

Twenty years ago, on the way home from the fireworks, I ended her tales of Speedy by saying, "We're like fads. That is, if we're lucky enough to be noticed by someone for a couple of years. Otherwise . . ."

"I didn't raise you to think such thoughts," she answered.

"Yes, you did," I said, and though I'd meant it to be a compliment, she was horrified, and I hadn't explained.

"To think you were a boy once," she says now, and I wait for her to say she won't reach seventy-five, using my age-of-the-country stats to start in on the cancer. And then it comes back to me what she said just before my patience gave out: "They've found Speedy—he was in Australia all this time," she said, and I mumbled the jingle— "Plop, plop, fizz, fizz."

"The little boy who brings you the best medicine in the world. You don't think it's important, do you?"

"I thought you meant an actor played Speedy, some kid in a mascot suit."

"Speedy's his own self," she said. "Don't you watch television anymore?"

But it turned out she was disappointed. "Speedy doesn't look good in color," she admitted. "He's got red hair and blue eyes. Those are doll's colors. And there's something about his smile reminds me of Gerald Ford."

Back then I was living in three rooms above a garage in Cherry City. I was delivering *The Mother's Encyclopedia*, driving into Millvale and Sharpsburg and Etna and Aspinwall, all the way to the North Side where my territory ended.

Every day I passed the Friendly Tavern. On both sides, coming or going, were enormous smiley faces, but that tavern, when the country was just 199 years old, had closed anyway. I thought I could make it into a restaurant, that I could buy it cheap and get myself started.

A few years before, someone had thought those popular smiley faces would bring in tired travelers, but I knew it would drive them away. Who would be willing to pull into a parking lot for a bar with such an insipid logo? It would be like pulling off to park in front of a porn shop, checking your rearview mirror to make sure you didn't recognize the car behind you.

One afternoon, a few months after it closed, I pulled around back, thinking I was going to take a look inside. The lot was filled with trash, beer cases and pizza boxes and a hundred other things you'd expect, but what I walked to at once was the burned-out car.

On the front seat, charred but still recognizable, was a rolled-up carpet, and the first thing I thought was there had to be a body inside. That car had been there for weeks, most likely, and I wondered why nobody had nosed around back there before, whether or not I should tell somebody, at least call the police. That body might or might not have had anything to do with the Friendly Tavern. I thought over a dozen plans, and then I backed away because I didn't want to know whether or not my guess was right.

That night I piled the three boxes of *The Mother's Encyclopedia* I had left on the kitchen table. It was time to quit, I thought. It was time to look into loans and interest and sites other than the Friendly Tavern. As far as I knew, aside from the copy I'd given my mother, none of the books I'd sold had ever been read by their owners. And the next day I stacked them in the backseat of that burned-out car, doused them with gasoline, and started a blaze of my own.

"Look at this for a second," she says now, thumbing through her volume.

"I'm beat, Mom," I say, but I lean over her shoulder to see what she'll show me in nothing but moonlight.

"You had this," she says, stopping at chicken pox. She reads the paragraphs I can't make out under the picture of a small child covered with a rash. "But that's not the way it was," she says.

She looks up measles, strep throat, and mumps, all the diseases I had and pronounces *The Mother's Encyclopedia* wrong on all of them.

"Those zizzits took a little while to clear up, but for everything else a little Alka-Seltzer and you were ready for anything."

"We put Alka-Seltzer into Coke, Mom. It was supposed to get you high."

"Did it?"

"I thought so for fifteen minutes. I took four tablets with two cans, but nothing happened except an attack of the burps."

"Speedy was born almost the same time as you," she says. "He's just a year younger."

So Speedy will be forty-four this year, and as far as I know, he moved back in with his mother during the 80s just like I did because he couldn't sell a damn thing anymore. The only way you can see him now is in a display case at Miles Laboratories.

"You take care, Mom. You get some sleep," I say.

"I don't need to sleep anymore. It doesn't make any difference."

After I close the door to my room I pull a wad of bills out of my jeans to see how much I stuffed into my pocket from the locker I'd chosen to rob during the second half of the basketball game. Thirty-nine dollars, not a lot, but I only take from one wallet and sometimes I get fifty or even a hundred dollars. You'd be surprised what somebody will take to a basketball game on a bus that doesn't make any stops except at the gym and, later, at a fast-food restaurant.

I could take a real bundle if I wanted to, but if I did they would come looking for a guy with a set of keys. I clean out one wallet, and they think there's a thief on their team. Some dissension, maybe, something that might help the school I've worked for these ten years when they play that team a second time.

You'd think players would learn to take care—I played basketball in high school and tucked any dollar bills I had into my socks—twenty dollars didn't slow me down any on the court. But these are private school kids; I figure they don't miss it if they are so careless. If they have to move back in with their mothers, they'll get a new addition on the house with separate locks.

Two nights later I decide to steal from the women's locker room. Something new. I've never taken anything during their games, and when I step inside, five minutes into the second half, I know why. In the girl's locker room everything is in order. It's like my mother's room when I open her drawers: I can tell that if I touch anything she'll know I was in there.

Right after my father took off for the last time, when I was still in high school, she left a bit of paper in her door once. I opened it while she was gone, and when I was leaving I noticed the paper, half the size of a stamp, folded so I knew she'd sized it to stick in secret. Not secret enough, I thought, but I didn't know how high she'd stuffed it into the door. I tried knee high, somewhere less noticeable.

Close enough, maybe, or maybe not, because later I saw two bits six inches apart. I measured them before I went inside, and then I put them back exactly where they'd been.

And despite all that I never found any money or photographs or love letters or even jewelry, which she'd stopped wearing and must have hidden or sold. I still open her drawers sometimes, just to stay current. I stare at her clothes, but I can't touch them. Though I think about what I would steal if I had to take something, and which nightgowns and underwear she'll take to the hospital with her when she goes for the last time.

"Where's the boogie man when you need him?" my mother says when I come home with twenty-eight dollars from the one locker I closed carefully behind me, wiping it down as if that girl would notice before she touched it and call in the fingerprint expert. "I unlock all the doors when you're gone. I turn off all the lights, and nobody ever comes."

"This isn't that bad a neighborhood."

"People are afraid of the dying."

"What would you do if someone broke in?"

"He'd think that I was stupid, wouldn't he, with the doors unlocked. He'd think that I was senile and expect me to scream. I'd get up and face him is all. Then something would have to happen, and for a moment neither of us would know what it was going to be, me walking toward him, making him decide."

"He wouldn't necessarily notice you were sick."

"Not unless he was blind. As soon as I lie down I feel like I'm suffocating," she says. "I feel like my head's in a bag from the cleaners."

"That's panic," I say. "That makes it worse." A week ago, after the first time she told me that, I pulled one of those bags over my head and held it there for as long as I could stand it, but instead of being afraid of strangling, I was afraid of the smell, that I was inhaling some chemical that would trigger convulsions or premature senility. I thought I could keep it over my head until I blacked out, and when I pulled it off I was surprised at how calm I was.

The bag had been over one of her sweaters. I wonder now if she noticed it was out of place, that she's begun to repeat herself on purpose to clue me in, and I begin to imagine a list of her ways of telling me she knows my secrets.

"That's the spread to my lungs," she says. "I don't need an X-ray to know what's going on."

"You don't know that," I say, but she's already committed to not taking chemo, and I think she is right.

"I told myself I'd rather die," she said three months ago, and the doctors hadn't convinced her to change her mind while it still might have mattered.

"All you end up with is a choice," she explained. "Take a pill and get sick as hell, or don't take it and have so much pain you won't be able to think straight. It's not Alka-Seltzer, that's for sure. It's no relief at all."

I shrugged and swore silence so I wouldn't blurt something stupid and irretrievable like "Good for what ails you."

"But I don't want to kill myself," she said, "if you're thinking about how fast this house is coming your way and how it will fit you."

"Bought and paid for," I said at once, breaking my vow.

"Free and clear ten years now, and the health insurance to keep it that way."

"And already two rooms closed up. Mom, I'm taking care of myself. What you own doesn't matter."

"You think you want to change your ways for me," she said, "but you won't."

"You don't know everything."

"I didn't mean it to be nasty. It doesn't take much knowing."

As soon as she said it, I thought she was right—everything I had ever learned seemed immediately simple. It was what made life so disappointing, nothing ever being special. I wanted to say this out loud and lose whatever pride I had. Wasn't that the way religion started?

The women's basketball coach is a real professor. "I think I'm the last of my kind," he says to me after practice the following night. "Even small colleges hire full-time jocks now. I teach anthropology. Sometimes when I tell a potential recruit what I teach she looks at me like she's waiting for a punch line and then, after a second or two, I know she's decided not to play at this college.

"Fifteen years I've been doing this—my budget has tripled—my department budget, in all that time, has gone up 25 percent—and this is Division III, no athletic scholarships."

He wants to tell me something, I think. Maybe that he realizes I am a thief and his hinting around will get me to stop. He's heard, like I have, that two teams complained about stolen money, that maybe the rest just kept their problems to themselves. He knows I'm around most nights. "There's not a thief on every visiting team" will sooner or later rear up like a great truth. And it will be followed by the correlation of "there's somebody with a key." I understand I need to get my story straight. Simple chronology. Time and place, which is all there is to excuses.

"You ever hear of Cargo Cults," he asks, getting me to keep the push broom from starting up the sideline.

"No," I say.

"They started in Melanesia," he says. "A hundred years ago."

He doesn't ask me if I know where Melanesia is, so I let him tell me the rest.

"Somebody had the same old idea to declare himself a prophet and predict imminent salvation and the end of the world. Only this fellow had a new scam: the sign that all of this was true would be a ship appearing, loaded with consumer goods. He gets his followers to build a warehouse, and when a ship shows up, they claim its cargo as theirs because all they're going to do is store it for use in the afterlife when the world ends. If they didn't help out, it would get scattered all over and be no good to anybody."

"And then the prophet gets his and goes?" I say.

"Something like that, but for some reason the idea was repeated again later on. A man named Jon Frum told the natives to build a warehouse and an airstrip because the cargo might come by airplane. He told them about refrigerators, radios, jeeps, canned goods, furniture, you name it, and all they had to do was build and turn to Christianity because Christians had a corner on consumer goods."

"So?" I have to say.

"That's what's puzzling about this one. The material goods never arrived, and Jon Frum disappeared, and yet there are natives who still wait for him to return in an enormous scarlet plane. They meet in a volcano crater to wait for him, but so far nobody's showed up."

"They might as well be waiting for Speedy."

"How's that?"

"The little Alka-Seltzer boy."

"Oh, him. He's off the air, isn't he?"

I want to tell him he should know something like that. That it's as fundamental as a weak-side screen, but I say, "Yes. The doll is on display in Indiana."

"Some sort of advertising hall of fame?"

"For Miles Laboratories."

He laughs and nods. "I should know that. Christ, one of my courses is called the History of Advertising. You can do a guest shot. Listen, today we talked about prohibitions. Tell you what—make up a commercial television wouldn't air, but don't use sex."

"Jesus turning water into beer," I say right away. "He stands there smiling with a cold draft in his hand. The pure mountain spring water this is brewed with reminds me of heaven, he'd be saying."

"Jesus likes his wine. He wouldn't waste his time on beer."

"He'd have to bulk up to sell beer. He'd have to get to the gym."

"But then he'd have to be on a billboard or in a magazine because TV doesn't do wine."

"Well, that would be a test then. If Jesus endorsed, they'd have to change the rules."

And then I tell him I'm starting day shift on Monday. To be home with my mother, I say.

"They couldn't refuse that, could they?" the coach says. "Cancer's a real respect earner whether you're a victim or a caregiver." When he shakes my hand I imagine him being relieved he doesn't have to turn me in.

Basketball has three more home games. I decide I have to slip into the gym at least once to steal. If the stealing stops, somebody will think of my transfer. And I have a great excuse if somebody finds me in the locker room five hours after my shift ends. "I've been looking for the thief," I'll say. "I wanted to surprise him."

Friday night, the gym quiet because both teams are playing away, I wait for the weight and exercise room to close up early. Students don't come in here after nine on weekends. So when the work study student starts to lock up, there is only a woman professor at the fountain.

She's been coming here since the semester started, always on Friday nights when only the geeks and the fatties exercise, happy to have something to do while doors open and beer pours all over campus.

"Could I ask you something," I say.

She takes two steps back, but she nods.

"My mother wants a poem read at her funeral," I say. "She wants me to read it. I know you're an English teacher, and she wants me to hear it read by someone who's trained."

"I'm sorry," she says at once, "that's not what we do."

"English doesn't read poems?"

"Not the way you mean. We read the criticism."

"It's Dylan Thomas."

She frowns and takes two more steps back. "May I offer a suggestion?"

"Sure."

"A woman poet."

"I don't understand."

"She should choose a poem by a woman."

"There's fireworks over in the borough," my mother says the next afternoon. "Why don't I pull myself together, and we can watch them celebrate their bicentennial days. Maybe there's good medicine in it."

"It's not the same as the United States," I say.

"Yes, it is."

An hour later, because I choose the newly widened state road, I notice somebody's repainted the smiley face on a refurbished

Friendly Tavern. Two trucks half full of trash from remodeling are parked under windows from which slides angle down. "It's good to see somebody giving that eyesore a chance," my mother says, and when I shake my head she adds, "You don't think so?"

"The smiley face was stale twenty years ago."

"*Forrest Gump*," she says. "The happy moron. He brought it up again."

"Revivals like that don't last."

"I had twenty years," she says, but I'm already turning and looking for a place to park.

She has the car door open before I turn off the ignition, and I realize she's getting a head start on standing unaided. I take my time walking around the back of the car, give her a few more seconds, but there she is with her hands braced against the door frame and her shoes grinding against the asphalt as if she were digging in to face a hard-breaking curveball.

"These Japanese sit so low you can't get up," she says. "They sit on the floor to eat. What kind of joints do they have?"

I take both arms and lift enough to get her upright. "Don't lay me out with any Japanese undertaker," she says. "He'll put me in so deep God won't find me."

The fireworks are disappointing. The monotonous showers of green and red, silver and blue repeat for twenty-five minutes, and then the predictable multiple shots close the show.

"Not even a pinwheel," my mother says. "Nothing in any kind of shape at all."

"We'll go to the Point in July," I say.

"Fireworks in March," she says. "I thought this might be a good idea, but it doesn't seem right."

"They didn't think about that when they founded the town, Mom."

"At least they could have set them off earlier before we all froze."

"We'll go to the Point," I say again.

"No, we won't."

On Monday I don't know what to do with myself at 4:00. I open applesauce and soup because Sunday night my mother declared she couldn't abide solid food anymore. I heat the soup and dump the applesauce in a bowl, but I can't face eating it, and it had only taken two minutes until I started to hear myself chewing while I ate my own food the night before.

So I'm lucky I can tell her there are two basketball games, the first at 6:00 because the visiting team has a JV squad, and I can spend two hours at the mall eating pizza and picking one thing from each store I'd like to steal, all the way from a diamond necklace at Weinstein's to a Richard Nixon mask at Spencer's Gifts, if everybody who worked there would leave to play basketball for an hour. The varsity game, when I get to the gym, has just started, but it doesn't take long before I'm sure I don't want to wait around for the second half. As soon as I don't have a job to do, the game looks so boring I change my routine and duck into the visiting locker room six minutes through the first half.

What am I thinking, not listening and walking right into the first row, where three girls are bunched together on a bench in front of their lockers. And all three are crying.

"Who are you?" the tallest one asks. "Are you security?"

"No."

"A guy came in here with a gun. There were only three of us left, and he told us to hand over everything that was worth a shit. That's what he said, 'worth a shit.'"

I smile and shake my head like some old nanny in one of those Shirley Temple movies my mother watches in the afternoon, but those girls are pathetic. They sit so close together they look like a lost litter from some animal that's decided motherhood doesn't suit.

I tell them I'll go for security, and I think that isn't a lie until I pause at the locker room next door where our team dresses. Nobody is inside. I check twice while I dump tape and scissors from a gym bag and start cleaning out lockers, taking watches and bracelets and necklaces and wallets and shoes, filling that bag like a thief who carries a gun.

If that coach returns, I keep telling myself, I'll tell him I'm saving up enough cargo to carry hope to the savages. I'm going to hire a pilot in a red plane, and he'll land on a runway which will suddenly show up in the middle of a jungle like those airstrips in *Chariots of the Gods*.

I end up with more watches and shoes than anything else. We'll be able to tell time in that godforsaken place, and we'll be able to walk miles of bad road in style and comfort unless the natives all have tiny feet and are so short they think a basketball hoop is as high as heaven.

The History of Staying Awake

A hundred years ago, a scientist kept puppies awake to study the effects of sleeplessness. He had them poked and prodded to stay lively, and it took those puppies anywhere from four to six days to die.

Hypothermia, all of them. Brain hemorrhages for a good many.

A few years later, another researcher kept adult dogs awake. He walked them constantly. The three he tested lasted nine, thirteen, and seventeen days until they died.

Again, hypothermia.

I look at my old white spitz sleeping on the kitchen floor and wonder how the scientists felt about the last survivor in each group. The foregone conclusion of it.

My dog is fifteen. A limp. Deaf. Otherwise, it's healthy. For five years it had my wife and my daughters to keep it moving. Now it waits for me to decide whether it's time to eat, walk, or sleep.

My father stayed up all night. It was good work, he said, making things that people need. Third shift at Glenshaw Glass—jars and bottles. Even with seniority he took it. An extra fifty cents an hour, and he liked the hours. "You sleep less working nights," he said. "You find out you don't need all that time with your eyes closed."

When I whined about school, he always said, "Banker's hours." The bank was open 9 to 4 in those days. School ended at 3:30. If he were alive, he'd tell me I was better off for having the bank I work at extend its hours on Thursdays until 6 and Fridays until 8. I approve loans. Or I don't.

My girls, two years apart, are grown, go to the same college a hundred miles from here. My boy was stillborn after the car accident. "I'm all right," my wife Tracey told the policemen and the ambulance attendants. Later, when I saw her in the hospital, she said, "The baby's all right."

The doctors ran all those tests and then told her that. They sent her home after twelve hours, and the next day the boy was stillborn. The girls were seven and nine, old enough to know. I'd had a vasectomy two weeks before the accident because in less than a month that boy would be born and all of the bad things that could happen to a fetus were behind us.

"No more gas in the tank." That was one of the jokes I heard at work during those two weeks after my operation.

"There's gas, it's just lead-free now," I said. The two new tellers didn't get it. They thought all gas was lead-free.

Nobody, of course, joked about the stillborn. "He's a quiet one," I said to myself when they looked my way at the bank. "I'm saving money on diapers."

My having that vasectomy complicated their sympathy. I'd had more than one death in my family.

The longest I ever stayed awake was four days. For hell week. For pledging a fraternity. To keep us up all night, we were subjected to push-ups, mile runs, and footballs slammed into our freshman guts. Hell wasn't all that physical punishment. Hell was sleeplessness.

We were supposed to stay awake for six days. In one old legend, Gilgamesh has the task of staying awake for six days and six nights as a means of becoming immortal. He falls asleep, and so did I, on the fifth day, tumbling out of my desk in French class, waking to see the professor standing over me with a worried look. "Monsieur?" he said. "Tu es malade?"

The two fraternity brothers who sat behind me snorted and coughed. "I'm fine," I said, and the professor smiled.

"Très bien," he said. "Bon. Ça va." I looked at him with the eyes of a somnambulist. "Dans cette classe," he went on, "on ne parle que français."

He'd fallen asleep at the wheel, the man who sideswiped my wife's car and spun it into a tree. He hadn't been drinking. He'd had the radio turned up so loud it would wake the dead, he said, but then there they were, smashed together, he and my wife, at 7 A.M. "I thought I had it made," he said. "Driving all night, and there it was getting light." Tracey listened to him at the hospital that first day. She quoted him that afternoon.

"That fucking asshole," I said, every time I had to talk about the accident and our dead son.

"Let it be," Tracey started saying, which made me want to talk about it more.

"That fucking asshole," I'd start up again a day or two later.

"What's done is done," she said, sounding, after a while, like an asshole herself.

We had friends whose premature baby had died five years before. They called, of course, and Tracey talked with them. "They want us to visit with them when we're up to it," Tracey told me. I looked at her until she turned away.

It was three months before I said anything about whatever consolation they were capable of. "Remember," I said to Tracey, "when we watched the slides of Martin's dead baby?"

"It wasn't dead," Tracey said.

"It lived thirty-six hours."

"It was alive when Martin took the pictures. That's why he took them, because he knew that baby had almost no chance."

"That's worse," I said. "You don't take pictures of things you know are going to die the next day."

"You see things wrong," she said.

"I should have taken pictures of you as you went into the hospital. See? I could say. There's our baby right before he died. Right there. See it?"

"Let it be," Tracey said. "What's done is done."

"Sentiment by Paul McCartney. Senselessness by God."

She waited another week before she said she was leaving. "You don't want children," Tracey said. "You want succession. We'll all be better off."

"How could that possibly be true?"

"You'll see."

"Just speaking for myself makes it not true." I stared out the back window, over the pine trees, at the open meadow where I sometimes practiced my golf swing after whoever owned it had it cut once a month. For nearly two weeks I could find most of my shots, and then I'd have to wait until it was mowed again.

Although I was only twenty feet to the left of where I looked from the deck, the view seemed strange and new, as if I'd never looked past my yard when I stood at the window.

"We'll come to an understanding about all this," she said.

"All this?"

"Everything. The baby's not just the one thing."

"Just?"

"The girls know this is happening," she said, "if that's what you're thinking. My folks know. They've made room for us."

"And then comes the understanding?"

I've looked up the current records for lost sleep, and though these things change periodically, I came across a man in California who stayed awake 453 hours and 40 minutes, spending much of the time under observation rocking in a chair.

It seems like a bad idea, rocking. A baby would fall asleep almost at once. An adult would surely lull himself into a stupor. Yet there it is in the record book.

I always face the same way on the deck. The lawn runs down to the stand of pines, forty feet high, all of them, thick on the bottom right down to the ground, the kind you hate to see on a golf course. The dog, which used to run away, doesn't even need a leash. It hesitates for the one step before jumping onto the deck, splays out half the time before it scrambles to its feet, and then wanders around the deck for a few minutes, sniffing for something edible, before it flops onto the piece of carpet I've laid out for it.

Last night, at 11:00, I took the phone and six beers onto the deck. I stared at that phone until I opened the sixth beer, and then I called Tracey. "It's late," she said. "I thought it was something dreadful."

"I know you're the one who answers the phone after 11:00. I don't want Robert picking up."

"Robert's lived here for six years. He knows when I'm talking to you. It's not like you call more than twice a year." She went quiet, waiting. I took a swallow from the last beer. "How are you?" Tracey said at last.

"I lend money or I don't. It's all statistics. I don't decide anything."

"The girls said you stopped calling."

"Two months. That's not stopped."

"They had spring break, and now it's final exams, and you haven't called. In college, two months means you've stopped."

"I could drive the two hours and see them. I could take them out to dinner."

"It's finals," Tracey said. "You'd be in the way."

"If I died, could they come to the funeral during finals?"

"That's cruel. You were always cruel," she said. "I just didn't know it."

"Nothing's directed at you."

"Yes it is. You say things so I can hear them."

"I never touched you or called you a name."

"That's where you're wrong. There's a face slap in your tone. There's name calling in it."

I moved the empty bottles around to form an X, stacking the half-full one on top of the bottle in the middle. "I don't sleep," I said, shoving the phone between my shoulder and my chin.

"You never slept. I don't know how you do it."

"I got it from my father."

"Insomnia isn't genetic. It's learned."

"Like father, like son." I tipped the stacked bottles and caught both before they fell, not spilling a drop. I kept to myself how coordinated a man could be after six beers around midnight.

"I mean it's a mental thing. It comes from how you feel. You're not at peace with yourself."

"Of course not."

"You weren't when we were together."

"You had faith. I had hope."

"You should listen to yourself sometimes. You should record yourself and play it back."

"Faith means you take things as they come. Hope means you rely on what's right here in front of you. What you can lay your hands on. Who wouldn't want more children? Who wouldn't want a son?"

I waited for her to say "Let it be." I waited for her to sigh. "You take care of yourself," she said, and hung up before I could say, "Don't you?"

There's a man named Al Herpin who never slept at all. You can bet there were a good many people who doubted his claim. A man who wants to be known for something like that has to submit to observation. For months, not just a couple of nights.

The referees were carefully chosen. Nobody Herpin could possibly know. They tested him at random and frequently, like urinalysis for slumber. To stay awake, the watchers rotated. They kept their eyes open so long they decided he really was the man who never slept, a category unto itself.

Al Herpin lived to be ninety. Some sort of sleep disorder. Maybe so, but what might keep you awake, once you've stayed up so long, is fear. Those ordinary record holders awoke again in twelve hours, fourteen hours, a little more. After I stayed awake for another two days, I slept for twenty-two hours. One man, after ten days of insomnia, slept forty hours. Extrapolate that coma on the graph of sleeplessness. How could Al Herpin, after so many years, ever allow himself to sleep?

The nights I don't drink beer, I crave ice cream. Something to keep busy with, maybe, but tonight there was just a spoonful at the bottom of the carton, and I cursed myself because it was something I never do—you eat ice cream regularly you should finish it or leave enough for a full serving—so at 2 A.M., I took the keys and trudged out to the van.

The girl was inside before I knew she'd opened the door. "I need a ride to the yarn," she said, pulling the door shut.

"The yarn?" I said, talking as if this were normal.

"The yarn. It's the only one in town."

She was looking out the side window and the rear. How she'd come up on me so fast made me think twice. There wasn't a car parked along the street. I hadn't heard a thing.

"I was hiding in your pine trees," she said. "I ran all the way here from the Meadows."

I had the keys in the ignition. She looked at them and then back out the window as if she could see across the half mile of fields to the Meadows housing project. "It's Damon," she said, "my boyfriend, he's after me. I'm Tanya. He has the baby. He knows my mom works at the yarn."

She was a machine gun talking, younger than my daughters, I thought, taking a second look at her orange tank top, the shadow, even in the weak light, between her breasts. Every question I had included weapons and alcohol, so I kept them to myself. "I saw your light," she said. "I just waited down there hoping you'd come out because I could never knock on a stranger's door."

A car passed slowly on the street parallel and below us. "Is that Damon?" I asked. In the darkness, from that distance, I thought it could have been Tracey and Robert.

"I think so," she said. "Maybe. Oh my God." We breathed together in the dark, and then I started the van. I wanted to be in motion if Damon caught up with her while she was with me. I thought about jealousy and moonlight, how driving gave me time to sort this out before I delivered her to a place where that boyfriend, if he wasn't an idiot, would get himself to for a stakeout.

"You show me," I said.

"The yarn's right past the Coastal Mart."

"That's where I was going," I said.

"And you don't know where the yarn is?"

"Reinhardt's, right? The clothing mill." I thought about who would be inside that factory this late, how they'd feel about spinning thread into gold at 2:30 in the morning.

"Then you know where it is. My mom does all their cleanup. Her and some guy who's there for heavy stuff. He sits on his ass half the night and waits for her to ask for help. She'll be there. Her name's Darlene. She never misses. She works until 6."

When we pulled onto the highway, she slid away from the door, turning even younger, so close beside me I felt perverse. "A man and a woman together like that all by themselves every night," she said. "Don't you think that's wrong?"

"Not necessarily," I said. I drove slowly. I decided I'd drive by Reinhardt's and scan the lot before I turned in. If that girl was right about manpower, there could only be two cars in the lot, maybe a third if there was a watchman. I was waiting to ask her, afraid that, if I turned, her face would be inches from mine.

I kept my eyes on the road. I passed the high school my daughters had never attended, the middle school one of them had gone to, and at the end of the complex, the grade school both of them had finished. "I'll tell you if I see Damon," Tanya said, the words coming from a foot away. I took a quick glance at her, wondered if she nursed that baby Damon had taken.

I paused for the stop sign by the elementary school. Once, late at night, both of us unable to sleep, I'd walked behind that school with my oldest daughter when she was nine. She held my hand as we walked, and a car suddenly veered across the parking lot, pulling up to the loading dock we'd just passed.

"Everything OK here?" a man I'd never seen before asked.

"We're taking a shortcut home," my daughter said.

I turned my back on him, but he kept his lights on us while we walked. When we cleared the building's shadow, he backed up and drove away, though a minute later, as we walked along the street below our house, I was sure it was his car that slowly passed us.

"Because it was so late," Tracey said, when I told her the next morning.

"It was more than that," I said. "It was as if a man with a child has become an ominous thing."

Three blocks after the schools came the Coastal Mart. I could see it from the corner. I pulled out. No matter how slowly I drove, I had less than thirty seconds to ask what Damon looked like, what his car looked like, whether he carried a gun. I kept my mouth shut for two blocks.

"There's my mom," Tanya shouted, sitting up, sliding to the door. "At the Coastal."

I saw a skinny woman in tight jeans replacing a pump. I slowed and drifted onto the entrance ramp, and Tanya leaped from the still-moving van, stumbling as she got her feet under her.

"Mom," she yelled, running now, Darlene looking my way, taking in her daughter scrambling from a blue van driven by a stranger.

I had a foot on the brake, but I was watching that woman reach through the open door of her red Camaro and lean slowly down. A woman working all night by herself would likely carry a gun, I thought, and sure enough, when Darlene stood up she kept her right arm straight down her side, and it ended with a small pistol.

She took two steps my way. "No, Mom," the girl cried, throwing up her hands. "He's good."

The woman lifted her left arm to embrace her daughter, but she didn't take her eyes off me. I thought if I started driving, she'd raise that gun, that she'd probably heard that girl tell her about the goodness of other men, including Damon, the father who was, for all I knew, about to swerve into the parking lot as well.

They stood that way for half a minute, Darlene listening and staring, the gun resting against the outside of her thigh. Tanya turned and waved. "Mom gives you her thanks," she shouted.

I leaned out the window. "OK," I said.

"She was filling her tank over lunch hour so she wouldn't have to waste time after her shift. Isn't that something? God must be watching."

"OK." From inside the Coastal Mart, the night cashier, a heavy woman wearing an orange smock, stepped outside and lit a cigarette.

"Damon'll calm down. Mom knows how to take care of him."

They separated. We'd entered the scenario for relief, but I couldn't stop watching for cars, so infrequent at 3 A.M. I thought each one had a specific purpose, one of which was transporting a man who wanted to blow out the brains of whoever had touched his girl-friend. One, then a second car passed. The fat woman's cigarette glowed. I didn't want to buy ice cream from her ever again.

When I got home at 3:15, I opened a beer and drank it on my deck. The dog stayed inside, staring through the screen door while

I worked my nerves down. When I went back inside for a second bottle, the dog skittered sideways, its lame leg buckling. It was still scrambling to get up as the screen door slammed behind me.

I put my feet up on the other padded metal chair I kept out for a makeshift ottoman. The glass-topped table listed a little, one leg dipped between the oak boards of the deck. I played with it, rocking the table slightly, keeping one eye on the bottle. It was so quiet I could hear the dog's nervous limp as it shifted its weight in the doorway and steadied itself.

There was movement among the pines, and for a moment I thought Tanya had taken up hiding there again. I sat up and then stood when I saw a man emerge from the shadows and start to walk up the hill and across the lawn. I was sure this was Damon. He put his head down and jogged up the eight steps to the deck.

At the top of the stairs he caught his breath and looked me up and down. "I seen you all down there at the convenience. Like a family reunion. I thought I'd puke watching. You think you're a hero now."

"I just did what seemed best."

"The old lady showed you her pussy pistol. I seen that too."

So Damon, I thought, had been parked on the street near Reinhardt's. Facing the Coastal Mart. Facing the way he was sure Tanya would approach, with or without anybody helping her. "Yes," I said.

Damon grinned. "Followin' you was easy, big man." He was as skinny as Tanya's mother, his jeans nearly as tight. His hair, short on the sides, hung down to his shoulders in the back. It looked like the kind of haircut you'd give a small dog, one of those breeds that snarls at your shoes.

"Anybody would have done what I did. The girl was frightened. She asked me to take her to a place she thought was safe."

"That baby's not a newborn," Damon said. "Tanya's seventeen, just last week. You see how it is? A young girl like that. She oughta know how crazy she can do a man."

I nodded. I thought about how prepared Tanya's mother had been for the unexpected moments. I had two beer bottles, one empty, one nearly so. "I'm twenty-four," Damon said then. "You see how it is?" I rested one hand on the empty. "You know I came here to do you harm?" he said.

"I expect that's likely."

"I wouldn't kill you."

"That's good."

Damon was nearly dancing, shifting his weight on the balls of his feet. "Not for this," he said.

I waited for him to evaluate the seriousness of my crime. "I wouldn't want more satisfaction than what I've lost."

"Satisfaction's a hard thing to measure."

"Yes it is. And there's you maybe fighting back. There's a risk in that."

He looked at me. "Though to tell the truth, no offense, but I decided, seeing you there with Darlene and Tanya, you weren't no big threat to me."

"I'm nearly twice your age, that's for sure."

"Somebody's grandfather. Tanya gave you the big cry, didn't she, grandpa?" Damon took a step and leaned against the railing, turning his back to me. I thought if I pushed off that table and lunged, the leg between the cracks would make it tip under my weight.

"Tell me," I said. "What's the baby's name?"

Damon snapped around, his hair skidding back and forth like a skirt. "You foolin' with me?"

"No."

"What'd she call it?"

"The baby."

"It don't matter to you then, does it? You know all you need to know."

He seemed pleased not to tell me, and I thought, then, that might help bring the night to a better end. I decided the baby was a girl, that this man would have blurted a boy's name, wanting me to know even though it meant giving me information.

"I already did you," he said. "I did you good."

I waited, heard the dog slide sideways and catch itself.

"I girdled your trees. When I saw you up here sitting like a king, I realized that's where she got to first off. See, looking from here, there's nothing all the way to over there—where else would she run to?" I looked out, but the field looked so narrow I thought I could jump it with a running start.

"You know what that means, girdling? All those fucking pine trees. She ain't never hiding there again. You think I'm stupid, don't you? I'm smarter than you think. You take one thing from a man he can see every day what's gone, every day knowing it's dead. It don't matter if he gets up and does whatever. He knows that thing is gone."

"They'll just go to sleep and won't wake up," I said.

"Yeah," he said, and then he walked right past me and out the driveway into the street.

In the 1930s, in Chicago, another scientist conducted his own sleep deprivation tests on puppies. He knew the previous results, but he had to see for himself. More humane, this man was. After several days, he let his puppies sleep, and they recovered, he says, except for those "that died without awakening."

I knew Damon was walking toward the far end of the street because all the neighborhood dogs, one by one, started barking. Earlier, he must have parked there and circled around so far below the yards the dogs ignored him. My old spitz, still standing vacantly at the door, missed the whole yard-by-yard extent of noise. It was like those old human telegraphs of ancient times, farmers calling the news of approaching armies from field to field. "Get up and get ready," those dogs might have been yapping at my deaf spitz. If they knew the history of staying awake, they'd have been howling "Sleep. Sleep. Sleep."

Piecework

Miracles were my mother's department. Rescue. Success. Healing. Everything came from God's grace, and she kept that faith through her two-year bout with cancer that ended badly the summer before my senior year.

"It's a miracle I've lived this long," she'd say. "It's a miracle any of us are born."

My father, who had to pay for her miracles on his janitor's hourly wage and the half-assed medical insurance he had, cursed the miracle workers—doctors and nurses and gods alike. "They could make her comfortable," he said. "All those barbiturates they have. They can't keep her alive, but they could at least knock her silly."

He was an expert on medicines. "They think a janitor doesn't know diddly. Broom pusher, they think. Mop-up man. What do they know?"

He researched. He was busy with his own medical condition.

He'd been fainting when he got excited. Anxiety, he said. Vasovagal syndrome, he announced, after a Saturday in the library. "You look it up," he said. "You'll see I'm right." And then he wrangled a prescription tranquilizer from our family doctor and made my mother as comfortable with Librium as he knew how the last two months before she went into the hospital for good.

I thought he'd get over his fainting after my mother died and he started taking the Librium for himself, but he said it wasn't a sure thing, that medicine, and it would take some getting used to. It hadn't done wonders for my mother, that's for sure, and he hadn't lied to the doctor about his fainting. All he'd done was his homework on symptoms so he knew, going in, what Doc McHugh would prescribe.

"I'm taking care of myself," was all he would say about his fainting, so I let it go. I'd only seen him go down once. In the doctor's office, of all places, and I was the one getting fixed up after getting spiked in track practice two months before I graduated.

My father didn't smile when I showed him the puncture just below my knee. He drove me straight to Doc McHugh's. "Those holes don't bleed enough," he said. "You'd have been better off falling on the cinders. You can clean that kind of mess right up."

I sat on the examination table while Doc McHugh poked around at the spike pattern. When he was finished, he asked about my most recent tetanus shot, and when I looked at him as if he'd asked me about the taste of baby food, he stuck me without additional research.

It was over in a few seconds, but my father was looking queasy. Pale and sweaty. Doc McHugh noticed, too. "Give me a minute," my father said, but Doc McHugh had him lie on the bench with his feet up and gave him five minutes.

"Your boy got the shot," he said.

"It's all in my head," my father said. "You told me that yourself."

Doc McHugh nodded, but I started thinking about X-rays and motor-skills tests. I thought brain tumor and stroke and then stopped because I didn't want to know what else might be going on inside his head.

You could say I was having trouble understanding anything going on inside the heads of people I knew. A week later, Dick Hudson, my best friend, fought Walter Kochanowski, whose name had just been lettered in ink beside the senior bench-press record. Five minutes before the two of them had agreed to meet, I watched Dick Hudson tip his milk carton back and swallow as if he were finishing another routine cafeteria lunch.

"What's the story here," I said. "Why the showdown with the baddest ass in the school?"

"It's not about anything."

"It's always about something."

"Then you know all about it." Dick Hudson looked like he wanted to loosen up by slapping my face a few times.

"You'll kick his ass for him," I said, guessing at what he needed to hear.

"We'll see."

I walked beside him to the first floor boys' room where Walter Kochanowski was standing by the sinks in jeans and a T-shirt. His younger brother, a sophomore who was bigger than me, stepped out of a stall and stared at me. "You can't go back out now," he said. I heard a set of shoulders, and then another set, lean back into the door from the outside while Dick unbuttoned his blue oxford and handed it to me.

Dick walked right up to Walter Kochanowski and swung his fist up from the hip, slamming Walter's chest before he caught a roundhouse in the ribs. And then they scuffled and grunted and settled into a minute of uppercuts and hooks, blood, I saw joyously, trickling from Kochanowski's nose.

I could hear a disagreement outside, a chorus of refusals. I saw that Walter Kochanowski's brother was holding a black, collared shirt in his left hand. And then one of Kochanowski's punches rocked Dick back, his hands dropping, and before he caught his balance, Kochanowski seemed to be lifting him with one arm, Dick spinning and beginning to fall, smashing the side of his head on a sink with the baritone groan that announced the fight was over.

Dick lay curled on the floor, and I thought about the choices I had before his easy jaw or ribs caved in, but Walter Kochanowski bent down to talk Dick back from the short blackout of concussion, trying to steady his eyes with words.

The discussion outside included, by now, a teacher's voice. Rod Ford—Dick and I had had him for geometry in tenth grade. The Kochanowski brothers weren't in the academic track. They wouldn't know Rod Ford's voice, but Dick rose and the two of them washed their faces in that sink as if they didn't hear "What's going on?" repeated into a threat. There was shuffling outside, a parting, I could tell, of the bodyguards, but Walter and Dick took their time buttoning their shirts, tucking them in, and slicking their hair back with their fingers before Walter Kochanowski shook my hand as if I deserved something for standing so close to danger. And then we waited for Rod Ford to open that door, standing in pairs, Dick and I in front because we knew we were the boys who would be believed when we lied.

All my stories are true. My mother told fables. She populated her stories with talking animals so she could pretend I didn't know which one of our relatives or neighbors she was talking about. No matter. She always arrived at a moral I'd already heard: "The fox is in the henhouse," she'd say. "You know what happens when the cat's away." If she had lived to hear about Dick Hudson's fight, she'd have made the two of them into rams who knocked each other's horns off. "They'd lose their heads if they weren't attached," she'd have said.

Only the stories about me had people in them. My father. His father. Her father. God. All the men she knew were bullheaded. I wasn't even that far along. If she had known I was at the fight, she'd have said, "Just because they're going to hell doesn't mean you have to go along." And she would have been right either way because I never knew where my head was, going to hell with the best of them, especially in school, where I turned worthless as soon as my senior year began, doing nothing once basketball ended except waiting for the time I could spend with Nikki McKaskill.

"You're crazy," Dick Hudson kept telling me all through March and April. "She doesn't put out." He knew. We'd double-dated a few times, and Nikki and I had left the car each time he'd started undressing Donna Adkins. By May he gave up. "You're going to end up a full-time virgin," he said, but he started explaining how his father worked at Heinz, how he had a job lined up there and his father could get me in, too, they were so busy. "You don't want your father getting you on here at the high school," he said. "Think of that, Billy. People you know seeing you scrubbing toilets. Old teachers seeing you wiping up cafeteria garbage."

I listened close. During the last three years I'd seen my father maybe twenty times while he was at work, but that was because he did his cleanup on the late shift, punching in at 5:00, mopping locker rooms, sweeping the gym and the auditorium and the main lobby that lay between them.

Dick knew I was getting Ds in physics and solid geometry. His grades were worse. We'd turned into the two worst students in the academic track, but when Nikki was around, he talked me up like a valedictorian. "She likes brains," he said. "I'll congratulate you on your latest A the next time we park, and maybe you'll get more than a feel."

Nikki was going to Penn State, happy to be admitted. Because Dick said so, she thought I was trying to decide between Allegheny and Westminster, waiting on scholarship news. Because I never talked about college, she thought I was modest.

A week after graduation I was dressed in pinstriped pants, a white T-shirt, and a painter's cap, punching in to do warehouse work. "Lift and stack," the foreman said. "That's all we need out of you. No questions. No standing around. Just lift and stack and always in this pattern, long and long, then short, rotate, see how, then long again, long, and short."

I followed his directions, stacking a pallet head high. "Good," he said.

It was easy. The foreman said "Good" once or twice a day for two weeks, and then he forgot about me because I fit right in. My father, though, in July, fainted at work, and his foreman wouldn't let him come back unless he took a full physical.

Doc McHugh sent him to a heart specialist. Heinz shut down for a week over the Fourth of July, so I drove him into Pittsburgh for his appointment.

Outside the office my father asked me to take his pulse. "Put your fingers on my wrist," he said, "start counting," and when I did he turned so pale and sweaty I pulled my hand away just before he leaned against the car and stared down at the asphalt. "OK," he said a moment later, wiping his face and following me toward the office.

A half hour later my father scored so well on the stress test the doctor declared he had the cardiovascular health of a thirty-year-old.

The next week, when she asked for maybe the tenth time, I told Nikki I still hadn't made up my mind about college. I wasn't lying. For all I knew I'd go some day.

I kissed her. We were in her room, her parents in the house like always because they trusted us. "Remember when Rod Ford gave us the lecture on piecework?" I said.

"Plane geometry?"

"Yeah."

"I hated plane geometry. I got all Cs. Rod Ford thought girls were math retards." Nikki sat on her bed. She kicked off her shoes and lay back across her new madras bedspread.

"Piecework wasn't geometry."

"No, Billy, I don't remember anything about geometry except being humiliated every day."

I sat down on the edge of the bed, and when she didn't move, I flopped back beside her. "Rod Ford asked us what piecework was, and nobody knew. He walked up and down the aisles looking at everybody."

"Maybe I was absent. Was it in February? I missed a week with strep throat."

"I learned about piecework today."

"Ford never told you?"

"He told us, all right. He told us piecework was being judged by the quantity and quality of what we did. Counting up our work to see who should be rewarded and who shouldn't."

"That's just another name for the nitpicky tests he gave."

"He said the world was going to hell because piecework had been phased out."

Nikki looked bored. She propped herself up one elbow and stared down at me. "At Heinz today I got transferred to a new department, and there were these women pulling chicken meat off the bones."

"Oh God, Billy. Stop."

"That's their job, Nikki. They tear off the meat and drop it in baskets. My job is to wait until they dump enough of those baskets in the big barrel I have resting on a dolly so I can wheel it over to the soup kettles."

"What do you do while you're waiting?"

"Nothing. Watch them, mostly."

"Rod Ford wouldn't like that."

I smiled. "He'd love it. I watched them going crazy with pulling so fast and actually running over to get the meat weighed before they dumped it, and then I asked one of the old women to take it easy, what's the rush? You know what she said?"

Nikki shook her head.

"'Fuck off.' She was as old as my grandmother and she said 'fuck off.'"

I waited for Nikki to say "Oh, God" again, but she just sighed and said, "Factory talk."

"I saw her talking with the other women, and pretty soon another one dropped her meat and said, 'Up yours, junior.' I didn't get it."

"Piecework," Nikki said then. "They get paid by the pound."

All that background for my story had given up the punch line. My mother would have had donkeys braying while they carried hundred-pound bags for an extra cube of sugar. "Right," I said. "The faster they work, the more they get paid. It's the best job in the factory. That's why the women are old. It's by seniority."

"Someone ought to tell Rod Ford to hire on down there instead of picking on teenage girls."

I thought she was right about that. Rod Ford had meant the piecework of punishment, too, how to prod us along through the public distribution of triumph and shame. He published grades on the bulletin board. He listed everybody by their initials, but anybody who could spell knew exactly where the rest of the tenth-grade academic students stood, and my memory was telling me that all of my competition in plane geometry was male.

My father approved. By November of that year, after I'd gotten an A for the first marking period, my mother said it was the seed of pride. "You know what the doctor told me today," she said the day I brought home that report card. "He told me measles is the most contagious disease he knows, but if he was a churchgoer, he'd say jealousy, greed, and the rest of the seven deadly sins."

I'd colored those sins in Sunday School. Sloth was fat, envy had a face covered with warts, lust had a full set of pockmarks. Pride, I remembered, always held a mirror and was headed toward the edge of a cliff.

While I was growing up, before her cancer, my mother stored medicines to use when infection came around again — eardrops, penicillin, antibiotic creams. The best remedy is God's medicine, she said, telling me to scrub my hands with hot water before I prayed at the table and cleaned my plate. She meant obedience, I thought, but my father said God's medicine was a synonym for chance.

I put my hand on Nikki's breast then, and she settled back on her bed, letting me lift her bra and run my tongue over her body from waistband to throat. I could hear her mother walking through the hall outside the door, but Nikki had her eyes closed, her hand on my jeans as if there was no chance whatsoever of her mother walking in on us as she rubbed me until I came. "Oh Billy," she said like a promise. "Oh Billy."

The first thing she said, the next time I saw her, was "My father says piecework at a place like Heinz is exploitation."

Dick Hudson laughed. We hadn't been in his car ten seconds, but he had a half-gallon bottle of screw-cap wine that he and Donna had sipped more than halfway down.

"Those women make more money than I do," I said.

"But that's not enough, according to my father. The company doesn't make the reward large enough to make up for how much they produce. They toss them a few pennies to get the work done faster by fewer people."

"Your father ever work in a factory?"

"You don't have to do the work, Billy. Just do the math. You got an A in geometry, I'll bet. My father says Rod Ford has his head up his underpaid ass."

Dick Hudson passed the bottle back to me. "Drink up," he said. "It'll be ten years before Heinz will think you're qualified for piecework."

Nikki laughed. "That's a lot of summers."

"Fall, winter, and spring, too," Dick said. Nikki looked at me. "Oops," he added, taking back the bottle.

"I'm putting off college," I said. "The scholarships didn't happen the way I needed them to. I don't have the money." Dick snorted, turning unreliable. "No," I said then. "That's not true. I didn't even apply."

"But you got better grades than I did," Nikki said. "I didn't know you in tenth grade, Billy, but I remember your name at the top of Rod Ford's lists. I always checked to see who was getting an A, making sure they were all boys."

"That was tenth grade. This is now."

"My father thinks Heinz is your summer job. He admires your get up and go. That's the phrase he uses, 'your get up and go.' He wanted to come out tonight and ask you where you were going to college. He thought it would be an icebreaker."

"Well," I started, but then I just let things get quiet, and Dick drove us directly to the county park, pulling off into Avonworth Grove where a clump of trees shielded the car from the road. I wasn't getting out of the car. I reached for Nikki, but she pushed my hand off her breast.

"I'm going to college, Billy," she whispered. "If I wasn't, I'd let you do whatever you wanted."

She rested her head on my chest, and I kneaded her back. From the front seat, Donna began to moan. Nikki pressed her face into my shirt as the car began to rock.

I didn't see Nikki for a month. I couldn't call. Pretty soon it was the Tuesday after Labor Day, the day before high school opened and Nikki left for Penn State. I dialed her number as soon as I got off at 3:30, trying to make sure her father wouldn't be home yet. "Hello," she said, and then I said sorry twice before I asked if she'd go out for a few hours.

"Sure, Billy," she said.

My father watched me hang up. "Good," he said.

"Maybe."

"See this?" he said then, holding up a vial. "Valium. It's the latest thing."

"More news from the promised land," I said.

"Your mother believed in listening to the burning bush. These are men talking."

"Right."

"That girl's got a head on her shoulders."

"Yeah."

"By Christmas you'll be sending applications of your own."

I nodded because it got me out of the kitchen. School was starting, and for the first time in twelve years, I wasn't going, but I was thinking that by Christmas school would seem like an old dream.

"Billy, how are you?" Nikki's mother said when she opened the door at 9:00.

"OK."

She looked at me so oddly, as if I were out of focus, I thought she'd been drinking. "That's good," she said at last, turning to gather the newspaper from the leather couch, folding it, saying, "There's always something to keep after," before she walked it into the kitchen.

I waited a minute by myself, hearing Nikki's mother open and shut two cabinets before silence settled in. Without the newspaper on the couch, the living room looked as if it were waiting for a real estate agent to arrive with clients. Despite myself, I looked back at the carpet behind me to check for footprints.

When Nikki came down the hall, her father walked beside her, still wearing a tie. He had his hand on her shoulder as they walked, leaning toward her to whisper something. For a moment, he looked as if he'd gone blind and was using Nikki for direction.

"Well," he said, holding out his hand toward me. "Best wishes."

"Thanks," I said, accepting his hand.

"Jesus Christ," I said to Nikki in the car.

"Everyone's a client to my father, Billy. It's not you."

"Sure."

"Our fathers are different," Nikki said.

"Different," I said. "Jesus Christ."

"It's just a fact, Billy. It's not cruel or arrogant for me to say that."

"Our mothers are different, too," I said, slowing for a stoplight. I thought she might open the door and get out, walking the half mile back to her house, but she turned on the radio, turning the dial slowly through static into voices and through static again. All I could think of was how cheap the radio seemed without push buttons set to Pittsburgh's stations.

She clicked it off and looked at me. "Billy," she said, "my father's just the kind of man who thinks factory work is for strangers." And then she slid over to the door and wound the window down and stuck her face into the wind.

The high school was coming up on our left. I pulled into the front lot, saw my father coiling up the cord to the scrubber in the main lobby. Nikki pulled her head in. "I want you to meet my dad," I said.

"I've seen him, Billy. I know he's a janitor here."

"I never told you."

"Everybody knows, Billy. I'm not special."

I knocked on the door, and my father looked, hesitated, then walked over and opened up. "What's the problem?" he said.

"This is Nikki," I said at once. "I wanted you to meet her."

He smiled. "Come on in," he said. "Make yourself at home while I get all this put away."

"We'll walk for a minute, Dad. We'll be back when you're finished here."

"Sure," he said. "You know where everything is."

We turned the corner and stopped at the open door to the principal's office. Mr. Tench, the lettering on the glass said. "Do you know his first name?" I said.

"Harold."

I slid my fingertips over the pocks in the glass that blurred everything behind it. "Really," I said.

"He lives on our street, Billy."

I pulled my hand back. "Would you stay here for a second? I'll be right back."

"Sure, Billy. Take as long as you want."

My father had the scrubber put away and had the buffer plugged in. "Wax and wipe," he said.

"I wanted you to see Nikki before she's gone."

"Think basketball, Billy. Think of this as an early time-out. You're still in the first quarter. You're just rethinking your strategy."

"Nikki's off to college, Dad," I said. "It's late in the fourth quarter—she's good as gone."

"You'd make a terrible coach, giving up like that with time still on the clock."

My father switched on the buffer, and I watched him swing it back and forth in the small arcs of a man who's been handling that machine for years. The shine he was bringing up would be gone by tomorrow afternoon, two thousand teenagers scuffing through their first day. I backed up a step, then two, and managed a short-armed wave to let him know I was leaving.

My father snapped off the buffer. "You want to make a few passes with this?" he said.

"No thanks." I remembered how I'd switched it on, two years before, the buffer immediately lurching in a half circle until it slammed into the wall and skidded along while I tried to get back in front of it. I'd hit the switch, finally, giving up, and dragged it back to where I'd started, but my father, coming down the hall, had seen the sweeping trail of gleaming tile.

"It's tricky," he'd said then, but I'd shrugged like somebody who didn't give a damn about janitor's machines.

"Let's go in the gym, shoot a few baskets before you and Nikki run off."

"She's already bored, Dad."

"She can shoot, too. Or she can watch for ten minutes. I'll turn the lights on for us."

Nikki was sitting in Mr. Tench's chair. She had the new school handbook shoved under the light coming through the window from outside. "Somebody else gets those tomorrow," I said.

"These rules are so dumb," Nikki said. "I don't remember ever reading them. We get them on the first day, I remember that, but what did we do with them?"

"I think I threw mine in the bottom of my locker. I'd find it at the end of the year and pitch it out with old tests and rotten sweat socks."

"I must have taken mine home. My parents must have stored them somewhere in case something came up at school."

I looked out the window, getting a handle on what Mr. Tench would see every day. When Nikki sat up, replacing the handbook in the metal tray to her left, I felt like sitting down in one of the two chairs facing that desk. "Dad wants me to shoot a few baskets. He's on break. Fifteen minutes. By now it's ten minutes, tops."

"It's OK, Billy. You don't have to worry about me being bored."

"His break will be over, and then we'll go."

"Billy," she started, but then she was out of the chair and through the door, so I was following her across the lobby.

My father bounced the ball to Nikki. She dribbled the ball so hard it bounced to eye level, slapping it as if her hand were a gavel. She held it with two hands in front of her face and fired it off the backboard. It caromed to my father on the other side of the court, and he brought the ball to his chest and pushed up a two-hand set shot that kissed off the glass and plunged through the hoop into my hands.

I fed him the ball, and he banked a second one through before he missed the third. When I turned and lobbed the ball to Nikki, I saw her lower her hands, holding the ball just above her breasts before she pushed it, hitting the rim this time, though with no arc on the ball it clanked off over my head. I jogged to retrieve it, dribbling once, spinning, and throwing up a soft jump shot that swished. My father underhanded a bounce pass, spinning it so I could anticipate the direction change, take it on the rise, and go up in one motion for a foul-line jumper that nicked the rim, nearly spun out, then settled through the net.

I moved back for my third shot, above the foul circle, and this one felt perfect, but it hit the back of the front rim then the back rim, hung there, and flopped to the floor.

"You two have fun," my father said, sitting down behind the console where the student announcers called lineup changes through the PA system. Nikki pushed up another shot, leaving it short, and I chased it down as it rolled toward the bleachers. I saw my father busying himself behind the console. Chipping off old chewing gum, I thought, and then Nikki came over to the water fountain, and I watched her drink as if I'd never seen her before.

"What?" she said, turning toward me, but before I had to say anything I heard the crackle of the PA speakers.

"Enjoy," my father said into the microphone, and then he was climbing the bleachers while Phil Phillips started singing "Sea of Love."

Nikki smiled. My father expected us to dance, and as he disappeared through the door, I took Nikki's hand and pulled her close, sliding onto the gym floor.

"Your father's trying so hard," Nikki said, but she relaxed against me until the record ended.

"Yes he is," I said then, but another song began, the Sheppards singing "Island of Love," and both of us knew my father had stacked those records, that they would flop down, one by one, until all the locations for love had been sung.

Surely, I thought, my father was listening in the lobby. I imagined him looking through the door to watch us dancing. "Lover's Island" started. In the geography of love, anything was possible. And when "Mountain of Love" began, an up-tempo song, Nikki stayed pressed so close against me I knew why my father believed.

But what he wouldn't see from that doorway was how I was holding onto Nikki to keep from dropping to my knees. When that last song was over, I was going to follow her like she was taking me to my first day of kindergarten, staying close until she closed the door on my stricken face.

Stacking those records seemed so unlike my father that I thought he really did have a brain tumor, that he was different now, that he might come back in here and wipe our small scuffs by hand, getting everything just right before the new year began, that there truly were miracles, that if we worked at them, one by one, we'd receive credit for the quantity and quality of what we wished for.

The Serial Plagiarist

Lou Rhoads was sitting as far from the door as his office would allow, but Susannah Grau stood in the doorway as if she meant to declare something important from across the room. "I'm in your class," she said. "Tuesdays and Thursdays."

"I know who you are, Susannah," Rhoads said. "The semester's more than half over."

"I have to talk to you," she said, not moving.

"That's something we agree on," Rhoads said. "But first you might want to close the door to hear what I have to say."

"Oh." She closed it at once and sat down so quickly and so close to him Rhoads thought she'd taped a suicide bomb around her waist and was about to blow them up.

"You've plagiarized a second time."

Susannah seemed confused, as if she'd come to confess and now the drama had been deflated. "I came to explain," she said, "why I've been missing class."

"Let's start with that then."

"I had blood tests done a few weeks ago. The doctor told me I have leukemia, and my parents have been making me have another set of tests done by a second doctor."

"And so you copied another story," Rhoads said.

"I know what you said before, but I didn't have a choice. I copied one that wasn't as good this time. I thought you might think it was bad enough to be mine."

Rhoads stifled a dramatic sigh. Susannah Grau looked so pale she might have applied leeches to herself to acquire a pallor. When she inhaled, she produced the enormous wheeze of the bedridden. "I think I'm going to be sick, Dr. Rhoads," she said, dropping her head between her knees.

Rhoads counted to twenty, watching the part in her hair. "Come in tomorrow at 1:00," he relented. "I'll tell you my side of the story, and then we'll work on this."

She raised her head and stood up simultaneously. "The new test results are due in three days," she said, opening the door. "Do you think this can wait?"

"No," Rhoads said, but she was already closing the door behind her.

Rhoads called the dean of students and explained the situation. "What's the procedure if I want to kick this one upstairs?" he asked.

"Let me check her file," he heard, and while he was waiting he walked to the door and opened it, looking into the empty hall. "She doesn't have a history," the dean said. "It's still your call on how far you want to pursue this."

When he left the office, Rhoads walked the length of the hall to take the door farthest from his car because the walk, though longer, was flat. Ever since his knee surgery, nearly five months before, he avoided stairs. The first three months, on crutches, taking them one by one had brought sympathy from students who waited to open doors and stood patiently to the side while he struggled past. Now, without the crutches, the stop and start of climbing stairs one at a time made some students turn their heads. The rest jostled by, and he was happy for their indifference because his condition was getting more difficult to explain with each passing week.

The day before, during what had been planned as his last appointment, Rhoads had argued with his surgeon about the state of his repaired knee. "It's five months now," he'd pointed out, "and it's worse than it was the day of the operation."

The surgeon, whose office walls sported three framed, oversized photographs of him completing marathons, said, "Progress is still possible. Knees can improve for up to a year."

Rhoads, during earlier visits, had compared the times displayed above the finish line as this doctor, arms extended over his head, broke the electric eye: 3:11.26, one read. 3:10.35, said another. The best one announced 3:09.48. He wondered if the surgeon had a goal of cracking three hours, whether he believed minute-by-minute progress was satisfactory. "I'm not optimistic," Rhoads said.

"You had significant bone and cartilage damage, Mr. Rhoads."

"But in the recovery room you said four weeks of crutches, two months of rehab."

Dr. Feeman looked past him as if he were evaluating wall sites for his next photograph. "Frankly," he finally said, "you're a textbook candidate for knee replacement except that you're so young."

"I'm fifty-two," Rhoads said. "What do you tell your other failures when they're younger than I am?"

"I haven't given up yet, Mr. Rhoads. You shouldn't either."

"What if you did heart surgery?"

"Come back in six weeks, Mr. Rhoads," Feeman said, reopening the door to his office. "We'll talk when we're less angry."

"Leukemia," Rhoads said to his wife at dinner. "Christ, she thinks being pale is a talent."

"She just needs an excuse," Marnie said. "You made them when you were in college. I remember."

"I never said I was sick, not once."

"You must have."

Rhoads turned over the layers of lettuce in the bottom of his bowl to search for a last bite of spiced chicken. Nothing. "You pretend to be sick, pretty soon you'll find yourself sick," he said.

"You can't mean that. You sound like somebody's great-grand-mother who's never been anywhere but church."

"The mind works its wonders both ways."

"You think your knee doesn't heal because you're depressed?"

"I'm not talking about this anymore," he mumbled, pushing the bowl toward her as if she were to blame for his wasted food.

A month after surgery, when Rhoads had recovered sufficiently to hobble to therapy, he took, for the first time in his life, an elevator for just one floor. The therapist's assistant had been so young he thought, at first, she was a candy striper, some high school girl volunteering for church youth-group merits, but the best part of his ninety minutes was the ultrasound she applied to his knee, rubbing the warm gel on with her hands, listening to him say "there" and "there" to locate the spots that felt most inflamed.

When she talked, she spoke of her parents and the dinners her mother prepared that she enjoyed the most. In her early twenties, she was heavy and likely, Rhoads thought, to become heavier. In twenty years she would be cooking for her parents, preparing the same meals that relied on gravies and stuffings, salt and the rich fat of cheap cuts of meat.

Three mornings per week, as soon as the timer beeped, he began a routine of stretching, followed by pushing and pulling with his leg, every exercise a modified version of something Rhoads could have ordinarily done while he was reading a newspaper.

During the last half hour of his early appointments, other patients arrived. A fat man who looked to be in his late sixties huffed through a treadmill hike longer and faster than Rhoads could manage after three weeks. "A knee replacement," the therapist said one morning. "It's wonderful how these things work better and better."

Rhoads felt sorry for no one except the Mennonite woman led in by her sister. She never lifted her head, which tilted slightly down in the posture of the enormously shy, and she could not seem to raise her arms. She walked by leaning on her sister and waited silently in her ankle-length gray dress for the therapist to begin lifting her arms and maneuvering her shoulders. Weeks after her therapy had begun, nobody mentioned the cause of her disability or the likelihood of the wonderful things that might occur in her case.

On the last day, after twenty-one sessions, Rhoads walked tentatively back into the waiting room where he'd been leaving his crutches during the past five appointments. The therapist wanted to give him a T-shirt that advertised his services. "Wear this when you start running again," he said, and they shook hands before the therapist disappeared into his office.

Rhoads turned to lift his coat from a hook and grimaced as a spike of pain hammered into the inside of his left knee. "It's hell, ain't it?" he heard behind him.

An old woman who looked as if she was about to spit on the carpet nodded his way. She had a walker set in front of her as if she were about to do a sort of mazurka while seated, using the metal bars for balance. "Yes, it is," Rhoads said, and she laughed, and then coughed, and then muttered "Shit's sake" as Rhoads propped one crutch under his right armpit for the long hike to his car.

When he flopped into bed after the news, Marnie surprised him by rolling over, awake, and saying, "You wouldn't mind it so much if that girl was just cheating."

Rhoads stared at the ceiling, adjusting his leg. "It doesn't matter what she's lying about."

"Of course it does. There are degrees of everything. Absolutes are like passenger pigeons. There were millions of them, and then they all disappeared before we were born."

"What a dreadful thing to believe."

"It's not a belief," she said. "It's a lack of one."

He lay quietly for a minute, and Marnie dropped into her usual sound sleep, leaving him to sort through a half dozen positions until he found the one most tolerable. He'd turned, lately, to watching television, not the sports and news he had always watched, but the programs that reappeared each week at the same time. Nearly all of them were appallingly bad, and at first he made fun of them to his wife as if he'd become a critic or he was doing some sort of research to keep current with pop culture now that his children were grown and gone.

Occasionally Marnie walked by and watched from behind his chair for a few seconds, sometimes as much as a minute, before passing into another room without speaking. She seemed busier than she had been when the children were young. He thought of following her to see what it was she did each evening after dinner because nothing in the house appeared to change.

"Don't stop if you're not going to watch," he said one night.

"What?"

"Watch or don't watch."

He could feel her hesitate behind him, measuring whether to pursue an argument. When she said nothing and left the room, he began to raise and lower his leg from the stool, suddenly terrified.

A woman whose office opened onto the same hallway called to him as he walked past the following morning. "You might be interested to know," she said, "that last semester your plagiarist was a problem for me as well."

Which student, he thought, had spread the news? And then he considered this woman's friendship with the dean, the manner in which they might discuss the problems they shared.

"A serial plagiarist," he said. "I'll keep that in mind."

"She wrote another paper for me. In two days. I allowed her the opportunity because of her condition."

"Her condition?" he asked, looking around the office for something to focus on besides his colleague's benign, expressionless face.

"Her cystic fibrosis. Didn't she bring that up with you?"

Rhoads nodded as if this woman were reminding him grades needed to be turned in to the registrar. "Like getting that good parking space in the faculty lot," he said. "The blue zone for the handicapped."

She smiled pleasantly, a nurse about to insert an IV needle into his arm. "I'll keep that in mind," Rhoads added then, and when he turned to leave, the inside of his knee cracked, turning his first step into the hitch and go of Walter Brennan in a hundred episodes of *The Real McCoys*.

At breakfast Marnie had asked him if the rest of the class knew about the plagiarisms. "Sure," Rhoads had said. "The first one was so blatant, I didn't take it through workshop, but she'd distributed it to everybody already, so they were left to figure things out."

"And this time?" Marnie had asked.

"I had her give it to me first. But somebody in the class had already found the story on a table in the library. It had her name on it and the date and the name of the professor, and there it was as if she'd left it lying in plain sight."

"What did you do with your copy?"

"I gave it back to her yesterday while we were talking."

"You gave it back to her? You made a copy first?"

"No," Rhoads had said, immediately uneasy.

"Oh Lou," Marnie had said, "you're such a baby about these things."

At 12:45 an e-mail arrived for him from Susannah Grau. "I'm sorry. My condition has worsened. Can we postpone until tomorrow?"

Rhoads stared at the message, and when nothing entered his head but a string of profanities, he hunched forward, clicked *Start*, and spread out a deck of cards on the screen for solitaire. His knee throbbed. Each time he sat in front of his computer for more than half an hour the pain resettled across the front and along the inside of his knee. Eating a leisurely dinner brought discomfort. In restaurants he sat so his left leg could stay extended except when he withdrew it for the waiter.

At 1:00 Susannah Grau eased into his office so quietly that she was nearly behind him before he noticed. He clicked *Exit*, but she stood looking at the empty screen. "You're like Jack Nicholson in that movie where he slams an axe through the door," she said.

"*The Shining*," Rhoads said. "I did this in less than eighty seconds once. If there was a speed test for video solitaire I might win a world's championship."

"And Jack Nicholson might win for most times typing 'All work and no play makes Jack a dull boy.'"

"The difference is I've published two books this year. He never finishes anything but that stack of typing Shelley Duvall finds." Immediately, Rhoads felt like an asshole. His knee clicked as he straightened it. He wished every disease this girl had claimed to suddenly bear fruit within her.

"I just got out of bed to tell you in person I'll be in tomorrow at 4:30. I'd rather talk when the other professors are gone. I'll do anything you say, Dr. Rhoads," she murmured, and then she left without closing the door.

"I've become weak," Rhoads declared at 6:00, opening his third beer while Marnie laid out cold cuts and potato chips.

"You say that as if you were strong," she said, and his expression made her understand his despair.

"Stronger than I am now, at least. Strong enough not to be weak."

"OK," she said, meaning it. "You can get through this."

"Not as long as I can imagine the future." He looked at the plate she was sliding toward him, suddenly sure that the lettuce had been retrieved from last night's salad.

"That's what's wrong with you," Marnie said. "It's not your knee. It's the way you take something wonderful and turn it to shit."

"God help those who foresee."

"That's not funny."

"It's a start."

It had taken four months for the inflammation in his knee to subside enough to allow any exercise besides the embarrassing leg-strengtheners of the therapist. Rhoads had a piece of rubber hose to loop around a post so he could pull and push against its small resistance. He performed, three times a day, a series of single leg lifts from his back and side and his stomach.

Rhoads closed the door to the bedroom when he did these, even after the leg lifts could be managed with ankle weights. The exercises were designed for the crippled and the old. He imagined the rest of his body adjusting to the lowest common denominator of his knee, collapsing into a horrible, hunchbacked shuffle.

For the last month, at least, he'd managed sit-ups and push-ups and real double leg lifts extended six inches from the floor while he listened to the screaming in his knee. They were exercises nobody he knew did anymore. His sons paid a monthly fee to use expensive machinery to accomplish exactly the same things.

Even the sit-ups aggravated his knee. He could feel something wanting to tear inside as he lunged up, and getting back to his feet was a careful ritual of kneeling, getting his good leg poised, then extending the bad one and pushing up and forward, finding exactly the right angle to rise without tipping forward onto his face.

He doubled his numbers. He saw himself not so much fat as flabby, as if his muscles had begun to flatten and droop like his father's. When Marnie walked in on him during the second week, he'd stopped and waited, staring at the carpet and stretching his leg while she searched in her purse for an address. "I'm not looking," she said, but he locked the door from that day on, and only once, during the month since then, had he heard her try the knob.

And because she didn't mention the locked door, he thought she believed he hadn't heard her turn the knob and stop, releasing it so slowly he knew she was being careful. If he asked, she would say she was being polite not to bring it up, but her idea of consideration was horrible, full of secrecy and planning ahead to avoid conflict. When his daughter, during her last year of high school, had slammed the door to her room and locked it as they argued, Rhoads had said "Open it" once, counted to ten, and taken it down with his shoulder. He'd stared at his daughter for nearly a minute, certain that if he spoke she would hate him forever. The following day he'd paid someone to replace the door, and his daughter, to her eternal credit, had never brought it up in the seven years since.

Off and on, perhaps once a week, Marnie touched him tentatively in bed, and he'd managed, a few of those times, to respond, but she was so careful with her body and he was so aware of her care that he began to avoid chances for sex. He came to bed an hour after her; he complained of new pain as he undressed. By now they seldom touched each other at all, and he wondered what she thought of his three-a-day exercise sessions, the weekends he spent at his office even though he showed her no new work. Any other man with his habits would be an adulterer, and she would be better off with any one of those men than with someone so self-absorbed and self-pitying he could not even initiate unfaithfulness.

Half the lettuce still lay on the plate when Marnie cleared the table. Rhoads opened a fourth beer and dropped his leg across her empty chair. "What if she came to the house and told you she was sleeping with me?" he asked.

Marnie looked out the window above the sink. "That's not funny."

"It's another kind of plagiarism."

"You shouldn't bring these things up. I don't know how you think of things like that," she said, not turning.

"I can do worse, but this one will do. Tell me."

"Tell you what?" She switched on the burner under the kettle she used to heat water for coffee, busied herself with a spoon and mug.

"Would you believe her?"

"Of course not. You said she's a serial liar."

"But you wouldn't know that. If she called and gave another name. If she asked for me."

"What would she do, say she was pregnant?"

"No, she'd say she was worried about me because she'd just found out she had AIDS, that she'd never bring it up to you except she couldn't face me ever again knowing she might have infected me."

Marnie poured hot water into her mug, stirred, and when she finally faced him, Rhoads slid his leg off her chair and sat up. "Maybe she's in therapy," Marnie said, sitting down. "Maybe she's trying to work her way back in the world."

"That's for soldiers to say, not liars."

"She's in a war, you can count on it—nobody wants to be a chronic liar."

"Listen," Rhoads said then, "I went down stairs today without hanging on to the rail. There's something to hold on to."

"Really?" Marnie said. "Don't belittle progress. Forget this girl. Fail her, and do your exercises."

"Dr. Feeman cranked up the operating room report yesterday when I told him how shitty I thought his work was. 'This is serious damage,' he said. 'We grade these things on a scale of one to four, and your knee has two areas rated four, and one area rated three.'"

"He didn't say that the day of the surgery."

"He saved it for when he started smelling the scent of lawsuit."

"But you don't have your limp anymore, do you?"

"That's progress."

"You can walk faster now. And farther."

"More progress."

"Well?" Marnie said, bringing the mug to her lips.

"I had a dream I was running," Rhoads said.

Marnie smiled. "That's a good sign, isn't it?"

"It was such a pleasure. I was running down the sidewalk."

"I'm glad."

"It means I'm permanently crippled."

"You don't really think that about your dream?"

"There's no other reason to have it. I never dream about things I can do. And anyway, I know what I'm going to do with the little plagiarist when she comes in tomorrow."

"What?"

"It's a secret," Rhoads said in his best voice-of-mystery. He'd just decided to extract sex from Susannah Grau. He'd work up an entire scene ahead of time because he was absolutely certain that she wouldn't keep her appointment and that he'd never see her again.

At 4:30, as Rhoads waited for Susannah Grau not to show up, he talked to himself, trying to work out the language he could use to make it clear to her there was a way out of her problems. He couldn't say it, though. She would have to see her opportunity and offer herself, and of course she would. She was a habitual liar. She could convince herself and him that she enjoyed Rhoads touching her, and later, if she told, nobody would believe her. Thinking it through was better than solitaire, but when Susannah Grau walked in at 4:45, he thought she'd been watching him shuffle scenarios on a screen.

When she sat down, her skirt riding up her thighs, he thought this was the worst thing he had ever done, and said, "We should talk about ways to deal with this. It doesn't have to be formally reported."

"I can rewrite," she said. "Not both at once, but eventually."

"I don't want you to rewrite."

"Whatever else you want me to do then."

"Yes," he said, and then he began to believe Susannah Grau was wired, that somehow the school had set up an elaborate sting because every comment he made in class, every movement of his hands, was perceived as a solicitation for sex. There was not another sentence Rhoads could utter and keep his self-respect.

He thought he understood madness. Not one word or gesture could prevent disaster. No memory or accomplishment could identify him as a man he could live with, and for one lunatic moment he hoped she would open her blouse and let him look at her breasts. Where the wire would be, or not be.

At least he would know which horror he'd arrived at, Rhoads said to himself. And before she could be the one to decide, he pushed off both arms of the chair, standing over her, wobbling off his wounded knee, catching himself, and saying, "I'm sending your case to Academic Dishonesty. You'll hear from them."

He limped to the computer, called up e-mail, clicked *Private* for her to see, and then turned his back to her so she could write the next scene any way she pleased.

After Rhoads sent his notice to the dean, Susannah Grau gone before he finished a sentence, he rode a stationary bike in the exercise room for an hour. He followed the progress of his pulse, the calories the machine said he was burning. It was nearly 7:00 when he walked tentatively across the porch and into the kitchen.

"That girl just came to our house," Marnie said. "She said she was sorry, that she wanted to meet me and tell me face-to-face. What do you think she meant by that?"

"Did she bring up AIDS?"

"Lou, it's one thing to make things up, it's another when the girl's right here and doesn't look like anybody who could fool you with a leukemia story."

"For Christ's sake, Marnie," he said, but she motioned to the sorry stir-fried chicken lying limp in the skillet.

"What did you say to her this afternoon, Lou?"

"Nothing. I told her I was finished with her, that's all."

"Finished with her? That was the phrase you used?"

Bad stories, Rhoads had told his students hundreds of times, were ones in which you could see the outcome before it arrived. It's what makes us put books down, he would say, for other things.

And in our lives, he decided, this is why we lie, no matter our resolve. The need to obscure what's coming.

Marnie turned and started to walk upstairs, and Rhoads tried to follow, but he had to take the steps one at a time. He wasn't halfway before she looked down at him. "You really can't walk," she said.

"I can't walk," he said. It was his own fault for working at his health so much people assumed he was getting better. You predict things that way. Soon enough, people expect you to be fine, and then they expect you to act like it.

Wire's Wire, until It's a Body

Coming home from his father's funeral, late spring twilight settling in, Ray Salter felt a small jounce just outside of Lewistown. "What was that?" his wife said, slowing.

"Nothing," he said, but Cindy pulled onto the shoulder, looked in the rearview mirror where nothing, he thought, could be visible but the dark. "I hit something," she said. "You felt it."

"A small rock," he said. "A crack in the road. A tree branch."

"No, Ray. Something." She put the car in reverse and backed it up a hundred yards.

"OK," he said, "maybe a rabbit or a squirrel. What can you do?"

"I want to know what I've done."

Cindy stepped out and looked, walked back and forth, checked both shoulders. A car passed. Another.

"Satisfied?" he said. "Some little piece of debris was all it was."

"OK."

Something strange, Ray thought, settling back into the passenger seat. Something to talk about with his wife at breakfast the next day, but then, ten miles later, Cindy stopped again, crying this time, and searched the road for the dead body she was sure was just off in the shadows. Five minutes he helped her look, and then Ray took the wheel and told her to rest.

"Maybe I should do the night driving if it worries you so much," he said the next day.

Cindy sat across from him at the kitchen table. She'd started a second cup of coffee, but she hadn't touched it for ten minutes. "You don't see well enough at night to make out everything," she said.

"Nobody's night-blind at forty-two," Ray said. "Not even down at Eyeland. I'm not the one stopping for bumps in the road."

"You haven't had a checkup in years. You'll hit somebody and not know it."

"Of course I would."

He reached across the table and touched her hand, but she pulled it back. "A glancing blow," she said. "A little quiver and they'll spin off into the shadows someplace where you won't see them."

"If you think that way you won't be able to drive."

"I'll be more careful," she said. "I can drive as long as I'm cautious. I have to get to the office. You have your own troubles to worry about."

"That's old news," he said, but she shook her head. Over a year ago now, in early May, he'd been surprised at the tenure decision. Shocked, he'd said. Everybody but the incompetent got tenure, he'd thought. Lousy teachers. Those who never published and didn't show up for committee meetings. He had decent evaluations. He'd put out a couple of articles. He'd hit a dry patch the last two years, but he thought it was the pressure of needing an article at a crucial time. It would have all sorted out. The point was there had been no black marks in his book—three adjunct jobs and six years of full-time—and yet the dean had called him to her office a week before graduation to break, she said, the news personally before the registered mail arrived the following day.

He had a year, of course, to pursue a new position. She was sure he'd find something suitable, but the year had come and gone, and here he was, the last week in May, eligible to file for unemployment.

"The old news needs to be updated," Cindy said finally. "You go take care of that paperwork. All I need to do is fit a pair of glasses, help somebody pick the perfect frames, and I'll be good as new."

Ray drove to the social services office, passing the college on the way into town. He wanted to get in and get out as early in the day as possible. As long as nobody he recognized saw him, he could stand it.

The line, he was happy to see, was short. The woman who handled the forms looked at his personal information and said that she'd see to it his checks were sent in the mail, that someone like him wouldn't have to report in person to receive compensation. An hour of his time and he was assured an income for another year. He'd need it, Ray thought, because if he didn't find a teaching job by August, any department head would know he'd been fired, and nobody would ever hire him again.

For the last quarter mile of his trip home, he could clearly see the police car in his driveway. From a distance, his house already looked like it was on the news, as if it didn't belong to him.

Cindy was alive. Unhurt. She was calmly sitting at the kitchen table, the untouched coffee cup centered on the smooth pine. The policeman was standing in the center of the kitchen, his arms folded across his chest, evaluating, Ray thought, the way he approached his side door.

"I called the police," Cindy said at once. "You weren't here, and I thought they needed to know."

"OK."

"Hit and run is an awful thing. I wouldn't be able to live with myself."

"Your wife believes she injured a pedestrian with her vehicle," the policeman said.

"Of course I did. I hit him," she said. "A jogger. Running uphill the way he was, he had his head down. I only saw him when I came over the crest of that little hill a mile down the road. I put two tires over the center line to make sure I missed him, but when I looked in the mirror after I passed him, he was gone."

For one second Ray was relieved. "He took off into the woods," he began. "He went back over the crest of that hill." He looked at the policeman for reassurance, and panic settled in. "Cindy?" he started again.

"He's in the woods, all right," she said, "but he's hurt in there, or dying. God help me, I've killed somebody."

The policeman shrugged. "I'm sorry," he said. "We looked for twenty minutes. I wish there was a better story for you to hear."

Ray nodded, and the policeman shook his hand, holding it so long he wanted to slap the cop's complacent face. Ray watched him get into his patrol car, and then he turned. "Christ, you had me worried, Cindy, but now I'm terrified."

"You don't think I hit anybody."

"Of course not."

"And now you're in a dither because somebody else knows."

"That's not it."

"Sure it is. You had a year, and you couldn't even tell your father you lost your job."

"Of course not. He had his heart problem. He didn't need me to make things worse."

"I think he knew. I think he sensed it, and you not saying anything made him worry more."

Ray looked at her. "I'll tell you what he knew," he said. "The last time we visited he had me walk with him to the end of the street."

"Where was I?"

"Asleep. It was first thing in the morning. We walked into a field just behind the last house, and he said 'Look at this.' All those years and I'd never been to that spot. There was an open mine shaft with a piece of sheet iron over it."

"I don't understand," Cindy said.

"Subsidence problems. My father wanted me to know there were abandoned mines underneath our street, that the next plan over had twenty houses with cracked foundations, three yards with sinkholes. 'You never know what's right under your feet,' he said. He had a map the county had given him. That's what he knew. It showed where all the mines were."

"And?"

"He said he couldn't read the map without his glasses, so he didn't put them on."

"Did you read it?" He thought he heard irony slipping into her voice. It made him wary.

"No. What difference would it make? Why the hell would he want to know?"

"I bet he looked at the map."

"He didn't need a map. He said as much as twenty years ago the people in that last house didn't want to pay to tap in on the sewer line when it was run because they were dumping their shit in the mine shaft. My father walked back to that house at the end of the street to check for himself. That sewer's still never gone down that way."

"Nobody does that, Ray."

"Everybody does everything. Like this tenure bullshit. They think they're doing you a big favor giving you a year's grace, but it's dreadful. Going to work every day knowing you're fired. It's like being in the stocks."

"The students don't know."

"The hell they don't."

"You're wrong."

"As long as I think I'm right it doesn't matter if I'm wrong."

She picked up the coffee cup, and for a moment Ray thought she was going to drink from it. "Come on," he said. "Let's get you right back in the car. I'll drive, and you'll see we can go all the way to Harrisburg, forty miles down and forty miles back, without hitting anything."

When they reached Harrisburg without Cindy once telling him to stop, Ray was beaming. "See?" he said. "We made it."

They stopped at a tavern, ordered beer and wine and nacho grande, sharing globs of cheese and beans slathered over toasted, salty chips. Ray ordered a second beer, Cindy another glass of wine. He picked, finally, at the onions and jalapeños, the only things left on the plate, while Cindy started a third glass of wine.

"You know," she said, "maybe I've always had something like this. I used to pretend I was dead."

"Every little kid does that."

"You're just saying that."

"Cowboys and Indians, War, you know."

"I was always by myself," Cindy said. She swallowed half her glass and leaned back. "The time I remember best was in Wisconsin, at this man-made lake. We were on vacation, and I was six or seven years old. My father, I remember, was really happy because the lake was so shallow. You could walk out thirty steps and still be only up to your knees. Another thirty steps and it would be just chest high."

"That doesn't sound like much of a lake."

"I liked it, too, but then, the second day, my parents went inside and left me there. 'Be good,' my father said. I thought they'd be back in a few minutes. I started backing away from shore, feeling the water come up almost to my neck. I couldn't swim. My father knew that. And then I just sat down in the water and let it cover me. I counted to twenty and popped up, but nobody was looking. I sat down again and counted to thirty. It was hard, but I made it and stood up. Nobody."

"You didn't tell them?" Ray said.

"Of course not. I did it once more, but I could only get to thirty-three before I stood up. It felt like my head was never going to get clear. I think I backed up a little more each time, and I could barely touch bottom. I remember thinking I was going to drown for real."

Ray pushed the last three jalapeños together, but he didn't pick them up. "There were people staying in the other cabins, Ray, but not one of them was outside that morning." Cindy dabbed at her forehead with her sleeve as if she were blotting beads of sweat. "You can disappear," she said, "just like that."

"That was thirty-five years ago. That's not you anymore."

"Everything I did is me. Not having children is me."

"You can't think like that and be happy."

"I've never even had one to lose. What do you think my parents were doing in that cabin while I was sitting in that lake?"

"This kind of talk can't help anything."

"They were always at each other, but I was the only child. What do you think about that?"

"What do you want me to say?"

"I've only been crazy a few days, Ray. It'll stop."

Halfway back, Cindy screamed. "Stop," she said, "there's a body on the shoulder."

He braked and pulled over. "Come on," he said, but she was already out of the car running. He walked behind her. He hadn't gone more than a hundred yards from where she'd screamed. He saw her slow and then bend down. He saw something dark and round and quickened his steps.

A garbage bag. "Well," he said, "at least you had a reason this time."

"Open it," she said.

"Why?"

"To see what's inside."

"Garbage is what's inside."

"Somebody could be in there."

"A midget," he said, but he pushed the bag with his foot. It skittered away so easily he said, "Midget dolls."

"Please?"

He opened it and pulled out a handful of frozen dinner boxes. "OK?" he said.

"All of it," she said.

He lifted the bag and let the contents spread out on the side of the road. Chicken bones, apple cores, some sort of vegetable gone bad, but mostly paper, thank God. She took the empty bag from him, hefting it as if she believed something was still inside.

"This isn't funny," he said.

"Of course it isn't."

"You know what I mean—funny funny." It sounded so moronic as soon as he said it he started to be angry with her for making him sound stupid. By now, though, she was turning the bag inside out, the last crusts of bread and greasy napkins slopping onto the shoulder.

"OK," she said, something he could agree with.

"Now what?"

"Put everything back in."

He thought about who might have gnawed on those drumsticks, what kind of person would be tossing bags of garbage out of a moving car. "Put it in the trunk," she said.

"We're not a road crew."

"Somebody else will see it and panic."

They drove a mile, and she screamed, "My God, stop."

He drifted along the shoulder this time, slowing gradually and trying to reason with her. "That was a tire," he said.

"It's a body," she said. "Back up or I'll run the whole way without you."

He cut back onto the road and accelerated. She turned away, gripping the door handle, and he kept the speedometer at sixty-five, afraid that if he slowed down she would throw herself out the door. Every time he looked in the mirror he thought of the bag in the trunk, how much room there was for debris on the backseat.

The next morning, when he refused to drive her to work, Cindy called in sick. By midafternoon he'd watched two movies and listened to her slap cards down on the kitchen table, playing one solitaire game after another. The thought of eating dinner on that table, seeing that deck of cards stacked on the edge, seemed unbearable. At 4:00 he started walking, following the highway, facing traffic. The cars hurtled by at fifty and sixty miles per hour. If one of them hit him, he'd either be killed or crippled, and for sure he wouldn't be staggering off into the woods to avoid any help that might be offered.

None of the cars seemed consciously to avoid him. Every driver, for over a hundred cars, steered straight in the oncoming lane, and he imagined what his wife would look like approaching him, going forty perhaps, straddling the centerline, panicked. A pedestrian would think she was drunk.

After twenty minutes he turned into the campus. The first two weeks following graduation, before summer school began, was always the most deserted, but he saw a physical-plant worker sweeping the sidewalk through the center of campus as if he'd been told there was an academic procession scheduled for 6:00.

"Hi there, Dale," he said. Dale smiled.

"School's out, professor," he said.

He knew the students called this man Bubba because he was fat and stupid. He did the jobs for which no training was required. Sweeping. Raking. Weeding. In winter, chipping ice and shoveling snow.

"For sure," he said.

"They'll be back, sure as shootin'."

"Right."

He stepped to the side in order not to disturb the small piles of twigs and pebbles Dale had formed along the curb.

" 'Fore you know it, school's in."

"Right."

"Have a good one, professor," Dale said.

"You too, Dale."

He walked by the building where his office was, but he didn't go in. Somebody might be there. He had until June 30 to clear out. He'd come in on a Sunday morning when he was certain nobody would be there. He never wanted to see his former colleagues again. For an hour he sat in the library, deep in the stacks, thinking he was going to research phobias. When he finally pushed out of his chair, he walked outside and headed home.

A mile from the house he saw her car on the shoulder. Cindy was behind the wheel crying. She breathed wine when he leaned through the door. "I thought drinking would relax me," she said.

"I backed to the end of the driveway and had to get out to check a dead azalea that tumbled over," she said. "I had a quart of wine, Ray. A quart. I checked the street, looked under the car, and then I got back in and managed to creep down to the stop sign."

"OK," Ray said. "Let's get you home."

She didn't slide over. She stared straight ahead over the steering wheel. "On the main highway," she said, "I stayed in second gear, looking for walkers, for deer and rabbits and whatever might flash in front of me. The mirror filled up with cars. Half of the cars that passed blared their horns. It's still light out, Ray, and I'm drunk and paralyzed."

She kept her hands on the steering wheel. He saw white spots where the force of her grip cut off her circulation. "'Third gear,' I said to myself, and I shifted, accelerating to twenty-five, then thirty miles per hour. 'Fourth gear,' I said, shifting, but I stalled because I'd taken my foot off the gas. I got started again, but only in second gear, sweating, driving on the shoulder, looking for a place to turn.

"There wasn't any place, Ray. In a minute I felt something. I didn't get out, though. I said, 'No, you don't get out for every bump. It's nothing.' But I slowed down, Ray. I drove so slow I had to put the car in first and just started creeping along the shoulder for three minutes. I don't think I made a mile altogether. And nobody paid any attention. Cars must have gone by, don't you think? This is a road."

"How long do you think you've been here?"

"Not long. You're the first person who's stopped."

"OK," he said, but when he got into the passenger seat, they sat there for two minutes, then three, and then Cindy crawled over him and flopped against the door.

"What am I going to do?" she said the next morning, a Saturday, neither of them needing to go anywhere. "I thought if you recognized how irrational you were you couldn't be crazy."

"I don't know."

"Isn't that what they always say? That if you know you're absurd then you can't be insane?"

"I guess that's not always true."

"I guess not."

She faced the front window, looked straight ahead so long he thought she was seeing an approaching army of zombies. She turned. "We tried for fifteen years to have children, Ray. When did we know?"

"Let's talk about what's in front of us."

"We don't have money for a psychiatrist."

"I'm on the dole."

"A week of that is an hour at the psychiatrist's. I can't tell anybody, Ray. If somebody finds out at Eyeland, they'll fire me, too. Dead bodies—it's absolutely crazy."

"Starting Monday, I'll drive you to work and back. On the way we'll look at everything you imagine is a body until you see how silly it is. Two birds with one stone."

"Yes."

"We'll hit bumps and circle back. We'll see the hole in the road. We'll see the sticks and stones."

"Yes."

He walked over to the window, looked out where he could see the dead azalea bunched against the mailbox post. "I don't know why I wanted to teach at a college," he said. "Nobody teaches anymore. They encourage."

"Maybe it's for the best then."

"The best would be if I'd never done it in the first place."

"Well, then, you're going to get second best."

He raised his chin a little, looked over the tree line to where the state highway followed the base of the tree-covered hills. When his eyes came back to the azalea, he smiled. "Look," he said, "there's the bush you had to stop for yesterday."

"Yes," Cindy said, "it's the old azalea."

He brightened. "Good," he said. "That's good. Say that when we see a bundle of old wire."

"I'm not an idiot," she said.

"Good," he said, stuck.

"A bush is a bush if I'm not in a car, Ray. Wire's wire, until it's a body."

He pressed his face against the glass. "You think I haven't earned the right to be angry?"

"I don't know, Ray."

"You don't think this is anger, do you? You think I'm afraid."

"You tell me, Ray."

He wanted to stop talking. His words seemed weak. He was explaining himself instead of being somebody. In another minute just being a husband would be out of reach.

"Remember how I called my father every night because I knew he would only answer maybe one time out of ten?"

"Yes."

"He couldn't hear the phone unless he was in the kitchen."

"That's how it seemed."

"How many times do you think I called that last year?"

"I don't know."

"I should have kept track."

"No, you shouldn't have."

"Almost every night—that's about three hundred. And sometimes twice or three times a night. Another hundred."

"There's no need for a total."

"That's what you think."

"You'll think that way, too, a year from now."

"What if I don't?"

"The 'what if' story never helped anybody."

They both smiled. "Cindy," he said then, "I know just enough about everything to try the wrong things."

She looked as if she was going to take his hand then, and he thought, "If she does, this will be over." But when her fingers, at last, brushed his arm before they settled back against her side, he knew she was closer than ever to never leaving the house again.

"Let's get you driving around campus," Ray said, putting his dishes in the sink after dinner. "Nobody's ever around on a Sunday in the summer. There are six speed bumps. You can feel what a real bump is."

Cindy wiped at the table. He watched her make three ovals with the damp cloth before she said, "Drive us there, Ray. Get this off on the right foot."

He parked in an empty lot behind a dorm. "OK," he said. Cindy slid over, and he walked around and got inside. "Take it away," he said, trying to sound jaunty.

She managed to reach second gear, the speedometer standing at fifteen. They passed the field house, the front of it glass enclosed from ceiling to floor so prospective students and their parents could gaze, as they passed, at the enormous room full of exercise equipment.

"First bump," he said.

"I see it." She slowed, and the car reared up and settled twice, thumping down even at ten miles per hour. He waited, but she didn't stop.

"See?" he said.

"That was a big bump."

"And nothing's there but a ridge of asphalt." She looked in the mirror as he spoke, but she didn't stop. "That's it," he said.

They passed the library, two classroom buildings, thumped over two more speed bumps. "Now we're getting somewhere," he said, and Cindy smiled.

"We're going all the way back around to your office."

"Yes, we are."

"There's a girl on the sidewalk."

"Yes."

"She's not looking."

"She's on the sidewalk."

Cindy drifted into the middle of the road as they approached the next bump. "Oh God," she said, looking up at the mirror. Ray stared straight ahead. The car, going so slowly in second gear, threatened to stall. "Oh thank God," Cindy whispered, "that girl's all right." She pressed the gas just enough to steady the car.

"We made it," she said, pulling in front of his office building. "You want to go in?"

"Not now."

"You should maybe go in and bring some stuff home."

"If nobody's around," he said.

"Nobody's around except that one girl."

"You never know."

She turned off the ignition. "Come on," she said, "I know you have boxes stacked up in there."

Ray filled six boxes with books while Cindy arranged photographs and his manuscripts in a separate carton. He saw four versions of himself, from each of his teaching jobs, lying on top, and then he walked down the hall to the bathroom. When he came back, Cindy had his computer turned on. "I knew your password," she said. "I thought it might be fun."

"It's not."

She clicked on IN-BOX and the screen filled with hundreds of messages, all of the files unopened, 328 UNREAD. "Oh Ray," she said, "look at all these e-mail messages from your students. And these memos. And forms to fill out. How do you know what anyone wants?"

"I know when I see them."

"Oh Ray."

"I don't turn it on," he said. "I have office hours, more than anyone else in my building. I have a phone. I walk around campus. I'm always here."

"But how do they know?"

He reached over and pushed the POWER button. He didn't need to close down any of the systems. Let somebody else take care of that. "What did they ask you to change, Ray?" Cindy said.

"What?"

"You know, before they fired you. What did they suggest you do differently?"

"Nothing."

"That can't be true, Ray."

He looked at the blank screen, imagining all of those messages taking voice and jabbering. "If they'd already decided, it could be," he said, and as soon he uttered the words, they sounded true. He'd heard about editors who rejected articles immediately, filing them by date, waiting six months to return them in order to keep from getting new submissions from failed writers. He saw his dated file moving methodically toward the notification date. For a year? For two? He tossed everything he hadn't packed into the middle of the floor and taped his key to the outside of the door.

"Oh Ray," Cindy said again as he pushed it shut.

A heavy rain had fallen while they were in the office. With the boxes in the backseat, Ray felt so strange he decided to take the back roads home.

There were a handful of houses, and then the road turned rural. He remembered enjoying the extra mile because he didn't have to worry about traffic. Alongside the road, a runoff ditch churned with maybe six inches of muddy water. Cindy grabbed his arm. "Ray," she said, "there's a body under that water."

"Don't do this," he said. "There's nothing."

She had the door open. He had to stop before she pitched onto the asphalt. "The last time," he said, but she waded into the ditch, kicking slowly to feel her way along. It was almost a mile forward to where the ditch shallowed and ended at the crossroads with their street.

"Nothing you want to save could be under that water," he said.

"It's a body. I can't save anything. I just want to get it out of the water."

Cindy pulled a gallon milk carton up from the water. "That's the body of an old dead jug," he said.

"Of course it's a jug. It's only a dead body until I touch it."

"You can't touch everything," Ray said, standing at the edge of the ditch now, watching her feel with her feet.

"I know that," she said. "That's what makes it so hard."

She fished out something dreadful then, stiff and furred, like an inside-out, frozen glove. "There's your body," he said then, suddenly glad.

"Take it," Cindy said, holding it out to him.

"Christ, no. Throw it the hell away."

"It's a body," she said. "We have to take care of it."

"It's a squirrel or something. It's long past being taken care of."

She looked past him then, her eyes flying open in fear. He side-stepped as he turned, bringing up his hands.

"Sorry coming up on you like that," the man Cindy had noticed said, "but I saw the two of you and pulled over back there by your car and walked back to help."

"We're looking for something," Ray said.

"In that ditch?"

"Yes."

"What, exactly?"

"My husband won't take this," Cindy said, extending her hand again.

The man took the dead squirrel at once and put it on the shoulder. "There," he said, "it's out of the water at least."

"See?" Cindy said. "That's all you had to do, Ray. Be civil."

The man put his toe to the squirrel and flipped it over once. He looked at both of them and shrugged. "Well then," he said. "Everything's all right." And then he was walking back toward his car.

Ray picked up the dead squirrel between his thumb and one finger. "What are you going to do now?" Cindy said. He climbed down into the water and extended his arm and flung the flattened squirrel into the woods. "That's the best I can do," he said. "It's back where it belongs."

They stood ankle deep in the water. "There's so much water," Cindy said.

"Yes, there is."

"That was a good thing you just did."

"I'm glad."

"It was almost perfect."

They watched the stranger reach his car, turn his lights on, and drive away. "We can stand in here all night," he said. "It's June. It's warm."

"I'm not that crazy, Ray."

His balance seemed unsteady. He slid his feet a few inches farther apart and tested his stance. His wife sloshed backwards a few steps, moving easily, but she didn't bend down to check the water. "See?" she said, taking another step and then another, almost jogging backwards.

Surely, he thought, she was going to fall, and he raised both his arms to the side to steady himself. If he tried to catch her now, he thought he'd tumble face forward into the muck. "See, Ray," she said again, and then he felt such a sentimental longing swell up that he took a step, lurched, then pushed off, leaned forward, and began to run, throwing up splashes of brown water to his calves, then his knees, and finally, when he accelerated, onto his thighs, soaking and staining himself like a child.

Rip His Head Off

"Jason," Aunt Peg said, "did you know that ants scream?

"No, they don't," I said, but she was raking the anthill at the edge of our yard level with the grass and weeds around it, and I moved two steps back to put more distance between my feet and the black, scurrying ants. She stopped raking but stood among the ants as if to show me what a sissy I was to retreat onto the Kresses' lawn. "You have to listen close," she said. "Put them right up beside your ear."

I looked at the ants, sure she was going to ask me to pick one up. "They scream just like babies. They're smarter than you think."

If they were so smart, I thought, they'd be able to say something else besides "Eeeeeee!," but I was keeping quiet about ant intelligence because she'd fooled me once before about them, the summer before second grade, when my parents were still alive. During a church picnic, she'd warned me that I'd be in for it if I fell asleep on the grass. She said ants would crawl up my nose, don't you laugh, because she knew a woman who ended up with an anthill in her forehead because she'd slept outside and let ants find their way into her sinuses. I was two months from my seventh birthday, old enough, she probably thought, to disbelieve her fable, but I started brushing myself every time I sat outside because Aunt Peg had finished her story by telling me that woman needed an operation to clean out the colony of ants that had settled in her head. "Our skulls are full of tunnels," Aunt Peg said. "Any ant would be happy to have a house ready-made like a trailer." For the rest of that summer, I stared down and saw how the grass teemed, how there were nightmares of ants that would explore my head and approve of it for a house. And when I walked on anything but the sidewalk or the street, I brushed myself like somebody half trained at putting out fire, not knowing to drop and roll, but not running himself into a cindered fool.

Eighteen months ago, my Aunt Peg moved into the house after my parents died. "This is better for the two of you," she said, including my older sister Diana. "Your mother and father wouldn't want you growing up in my apartment on the North Side," and I was happy with that choice because Aunt Peg told us stories about her old neighborhood, making it sound as if she was lucky to be alive. "You can't go out after dark," she said. "You can't go out by yourself." Her neighborhood sounded like Lake Worthy at the church camp I attended each summer—we could never swim after dark, and even in full daylight we couldn't stray more than an arm's length from somebody who'd pledged to stay beside us in return.

The plane crash that killed my parents on November 1, 1955, had made them famous for a few weeks because it turned out there was a bomb on the plane, that it hadn't just blown up because something went wrong with the engines. Nobody had ever heard of such a thing, Aunt Peg said. She hoped they'd shoot the man who confessed. Better yet, she hoped they'd blow him up on television to show people what you deserved if you exploded a plane full of passengers. "Insurance," Aunt Peg said. "That son of a bitch wanted to cash in on his own mother's policy."

After a year, the story of the bombing returned like a holiday. When a reporter drove up, Aunt Peg did all the talking. She said she still wished somebody would go ahead and rip the head right off that bomber, but since that was none of her business, she was doing the best she could to raise her sister's two orphans. A man took a picture of me and Diana that was published with the caption: "Tragedy's Children." The same photographs of my parents were in the newspaper again—my father's picture taken six years before the explosion, my mother's only a month before, so he looked more like a younger brother than a husband.

After the reporter left, Aunt Peg said, "I could have told him anything. All he wanted was to take your picture. The two of you—The Bobbsey Twins Don't Go to the Orphanage. He just needed words to fill in the space around your faces."

"I remember that guy," Diana said, as if it was special not to have amnesia. "He was here last year when there was a crowd."

As our second summer with Aunt Peg began, I wasn't worried about being an orphan; I was panicked about being skinny and getting polio. I was going to be thirteen in September, but I looked like I was ten. I didn't have my polio shots, and neither did Diana, who was fourteen and looked like she was seventeen. I was sure my parents had planned on getting us our shots before summer started the year before, but Aunt Peg had said, "Not just yet" for a year because she said we needed to wait and see if Salk's miracle drug had side effects. "You don't just put things in your body like that," she said. And now it was summer again, the second polio season Diana and I had lived with her in Adams Park.

What's more, Aunt Peg had found out about the cases of polio— "More than a hundred," she said—caused by a company fouling up the way they made the vaccine. Somebody had failed to inactivate the polio virus. "See?" Aunt Peg said. "See what I mean? There's always somebody who gets it wrong before everybody pays attention." Aunt Peg said the company's name—Cutter Laboratories—so often, neither Diana nor I had brought it up all winter. But now it was summer again, and everybody I knew had had their shots for at least a year.

Aunt Peg told me I worried too much. "How many boys do you know who have polio?" she said, and when I answered "One," she said, "Listen to yourself," and I was glad she didn't think to ask me about my fear of flies, why I flurried my hands when they settled near me because my mother had told me once they carried polio from the filth they lived in.

I blamed Aunt Peg and her story about the ants moving into the sinus trailer court. Two years ago, even when I heard my mother talking softly to my father about "the epidemic," I'd eaten food that flies had crawled on because every boy I knew did, and not one of them had a polio shot. If I was getting polio, so were my friends, but now all those boys had their shots, and I needed to do everything I could to protect myself because I'd be the only crippled boy in eighth grade if that virus found a home in me.

All I could do was ask Aunt Peg about the shots every week, and so far, all I could manage to do about being skinny was watching Stuart Kress lift weights and thinking about what might happen if I spent an hour every day working out with him. "You should get a set like this," Stuart said, after his father had given the weights to him for his thirteenth birthday in April. The weights were black and round and small, but right off, the first time I started to pick up the largest with one hand, I had to regrip with both hands and then hold it as casually as I could, reading the letters and numbers of York Barbells's code for half a minute as if I wasn't straining not to drop it on my foot.

By the end of school he'd been lifting for two months, and I kept saying "No" when he asked me to try because once, when Stuart was upstairs, I'd tried the empty bar, figuring it for lighter than the twenty-five pound weight, and it was all I could do to lift it. I felt like I had polio. I started doing push-ups and pull-ups. I gave myself until the end of June to make sure I could at least lift the bar with something attached to it.

For pull-ups, I had to go outside near that leveled anthill to where my mother's old clothes posts stood like miniature telephone poles. The cross bars were thin enough for my hands to grip, and the forsythia bushes were tall enough, I hoped, so Stuart couldn't see me exercising from his bedroom window. But I did push-ups whenever I thought about it. I dropped to the floor in the middle of reading and did twenty. At least until Diana stood in the doorway one afternoon, saying "Push-up boy. You better be doing a thousand a day if you think you're going to be somebody besides 'the beanpole.'"

"You'll see," I said, but I was wishing I'd closed the door and locked it because I knew she'd been watching me struggle out the last three push-ups as if I had a hundred pounds strapped across my back. "I'll look different by the end of the summer."

She laughed, and I thought she'd been watching the whole time, knew that I'd only managed seventeen, a number so awkward it could only mean failure to finish a set. "No, you won't. You'll be like one of those Winky pictures Dad used to bring home. Remember those stupid things?"

I remembered. They were like the shortest movies in the world. The pictures shifted if you turned them or moved your head—a dog sat and then jumped; Mona Lisa smiled and then frowned. I loved them.

Diana grinned so much like a storybook animal I shivered. "People will see you, but they'll remember how you look now. You've been skinny so long, you'll switch back to beanpole as soon as they look away."

"Whatever you say," I managed, but I didn't believe her. She'd been skinny and flat the year before, and now she had breasts I never forgot when I looked away.

A week after I started exercising, Dwight Ware, who lived three houses from me, nearly at the end of the street, brought his new set of July's horror comic books to Stuart's. "Look at these," Dwight said. "A whole bunch of heads get ripped right off." Stuart told him to stuff a cork in it, but he grabbed one of those comics, and so did I, and we settled in to read, passing the three around until we'd finished all of them. A stake through the heart, a hail of bullets, a pool full of piranhas—every story had some kind of slaughter, but Dwight was right: Somebody got his head ripped off in each of those comic books—two men and one woman. What's more, on the back cover of all three was an ad for Joe Bonomo's secret vibro-power technique for building up skinny guys.

I was just wasting time waiting for Stuart to finish, but when he saw me reading the ad, Dwight said, "It's really cool. I've been doing the exercises for a month." Dwight was already thirteen, but he was as skinny as I was. I knew he wasn't going to make a muscle like Stuart did every time he finished a set of curls.

"That Joe Bonomo stuff is for fairies," Stuart said to Dwight. "All that pushing and pressing. You know what that's all about."

"I bet I can lift more than Jason," Dwight said. "I bet he's the fairy."

"I bet you're a queer no matter how much you lift," I said, but when Stuart said, "Let's see," I was glad I'd been doing push-ups and keeping it to myself, because after Dwight managed to get the bar up over his head four times with five pounds on either side, so did I.

"There," I said, but Dwight put on two more five-pound weights and squeezed out three repetitions. "Joe Bonomo's psycho-power," he said, letting the weights go before they reached the floor so that Stuart said "Jesus Christ" and checked to see if the tile had cracked.

I wished he'd broken something so Stuart would punch him and forget about the contest, but the floor was unmarked, and I could only lift the new weight over my head once.

"Jason's the fairy," Dwight yelled.

"You're older," I said, suddenly sure my age was my handicap.

"That doesn't matter," Stuart said, but when Dwight laughed, his voice cracking into a soprano shriek, Stuart said, "Wait a minute. You've been doing that Bonomo crap for who knows how long. You guys are so close, let's find out what works. Jason can use my barbells, and whoever lifts the least by the day of the All-Star Game is the all-time major league queer."

"OK," I said at once, but Dwight looked like he'd been caught cheating on an arithmetic test, and when I asked him if I could borrow the comic books to read them again, he hesitated like he thought I was going to send away for Bonomo's secrets of cosmic breathing and vibro-pressure, doubling up on him by using both ways at once.

I held out my hand, but Dwight shuffled them like he was trying to decide something important. Finally, he handed me the one with a werewolf attacking a woman on the cover. "Just one," he said. "And you give it back by noon tomorrow, no wrinkles."

"No wrinkles," Stuart said in a voice so high pitched I vowed to do a thousand push-ups every day.

An hour later I was sitting on my bed, through with reading all the stories a second time, but still looking at the Joe Bonomo ad as if the pictures would make my muscles grow. Aunt Peg knocked on my open door. "What's this?" she said, looking over my shoulder from the doorway. "You having trouble at school?"

I waited for her to tell me what she wanted, but she held out her hand, and I let her look. "It's Dwight's," I said, saying something I could hear Stuart repeating in that high soprano, but she thumbed through so quickly I relaxed until she held up the page where a giant praying mantis carried a man's torn-off head in its mouth. "The mantis got huge from an atom bomb test," I explained.

"Rubbish," she said. "You fill up your head with this and there won't be enough room in there for what you need to know." She kept the comic book open to the picture of the screaming, bloody head. "They're almost finished with that atomic power plant in Shippensport," she said. "It's not the bomb you have to worry about when you live downwind from that. You and your sister don't know what you're in for."

She tossed the comic book onto the bed, and it landed with a page folded over. I reached fast, smoothing it. "You'll grow up soon enough," Aunt Peg said. "You'll get bigger than any praying mantis. If they ever let that son-of-a-bitch bomber out of jail, you can rip his head off for him. I'd like to hear him scream."

I nodded and meant it because I wanted to do that for sure, but I thought about what you'd be able to say if your head was torn off, whether you could talk at all, and I decided, looking at the man's wide-open mouth, that you couldn't. You needed air for that, but I thought you'd be able to see your body for a few seconds, know what had happened to you.

"Until then," she said, "if somebody tries to take advantage, you don't back down."

I nodded again. I had never been in a fight and had never seen anything happen in one except boys pushing and shoving and calling each other names. "OK," I said, and Aunt Peg made that sound like she always did, between a click and a hiss. "I mean it," she said. "You make sure that pantywaist gets what's coming to him."

Pantywaist was Aunt Peg's worst name for somebody. The bomber. The fat policeman who drove up and down our street twice a day. The doctor my mother had chosen but Aunt Peg refused to take us to. I'd been meaning to look it up in the dictionary since she'd said, when I asked her, "A pantywaist is a pantywaist."

Mrs. Ware, when I brought it up, said she'd never heard of the word, but it sounded like something you shouldn't say out loud. Mrs. Kress said a pantywaist was a sissy, but I already knew it was worse than a sissy, like queer was worse than fairy. I thought Mr. Kress and Mr. Ware would know, but I was afraid they'd say, "Who do you know who's a pantywaist," asking as if they'd learned something awful about me.

Ten minutes after Aunt Peg left my room without saying why she'd knocked, Stuart called to say it was time to lift, but I told him

I couldn't come over, sounding, I was sure, exactly like a pantywaist. "You'll be the fairy in three weeks," he said.

"I have things I have to do," I said.

"Sure you do."

"One day won't matter. I'm doing push-ups."

"Push-ups? Start with the weights tonight or else forget about it."

"Tomorrow," I said, trying to keep my voice low and calm.

Stuart laughed. "I'll tell Dwight you're not lifting, and maybe he'll stop doing that fairy workout."

I checked Dwight every day, but he never looked bigger or stronger. Mornings and afternoons I did push-ups in my room with the door locked. And then, after dark every night I walked outside and did pull-ups on the clothes post, telling myself this could change me the same way Stuart's weights or Joe Bonomo's silly exercises could. The week before the All-Star Game, Stuart called after I finished my pull-ups. "Monkey boy," he said, and then he hung up.

So for a week I used the clothes post in the afternoon, did more push-ups at night, and when Stuart called two days before the game, he said, "Don't do any exercises tomorrow. Trust me. You'll do better with the weights that way."

Mrs. Kress had Tuesdays off from her job at Woolworth's, and during the national anthem before the All-Star Game, she walked into the living room in her husband's old baseball uniform. It said "Lynchburg" on the front and "36" on the back, and she stood at attention with the cap over her heart until the song ended. Dwight and I clapped for her, but Stuart made the kind of face I put on when I walked into church each Sunday with Aunt Peg. I watched Mrs. Kress through the top half of the first inning and wished my father had played baseball instead of being a quality control expert.

That's why he was flying with my mother from Denver. He could take her along on his trips once a year, and she wanted to see the Rocky Mountains.

The game took a long time because they changed pitchers so often. Dwight left in the fourth inning, and Stuart nudged me. "There goes Joe Bonomo," he whispered, but halfway through the fifth inning Dwight came back with candy bars for all of us.

In the seventh inning Dwight left again, but when the eighth inning ended and he hadn't come back, Stuart said, "Push and press, then make a mess," and this time I laughed so loud Mrs. Kress said, "All that sugar makes you silly." She cheered every time the National League got a hit and kept the uniform on even after the game ended and Dwight, as if he'd been listening to it on the radio, walked back in with a new set of horror comics.

"The August issues," he said. "They're just out."

"You're stalling," Stuart said, but he grabbed the one with a cover that showed a woman being dangled over a cliff by a man wearing a skull mask, and so we were sitting in the living room reading, Mrs. Kress cooking dinner in the baseball uniform, when Mr. Kress came home from work.

She modeled it for him, strutting across the living room. "It's not yours to wear," Mr. Kress said.

"What's the harm? The boys liked it. They think it's great you played professional baseball."

"In Lynchburg. Where the fuck is that?"

"Virginia," she said. "It's not a sin. Nobody cares whether you hit three hundred. It's having the uniform that counts."

"Everybody's wrong," Mr. Kress said. "It was one season. It was years ago."

"That's right. It's just a costume now. It's like an old prom dress."

Mr. Kress twisted the afternoon newspaper in his hands, and I thought, watching the front page separate, that he'd stolen the uniform when he was released. "You look like a dyke in that thing," he said.

"Good for you, Louie. In front of the boys. That'll teach them. Maybe they'll want to be just like you when they grow up."

"You old cunt," he said then, the words running together but so clear there was no pretending he'd said anything else.

I didn't turn my head. I was afraid if I looked at Stuart he'd punch me for listening. "OK, Louie," she said. "Here, take it," and she unbuttoned the shirt, shook out of it, and flung it at him. He blocked it with one arm, and it hung there like his elbow was a doorknob. I tried not to look at Mrs. Kress's white bra, but when she started to step out of the uniform pants, Mr. Kress jerked his arm and dropped the shirt before he left the room.

I headed for the door, and Dwight followed, tugging the comic book out of Stuart's hand in a way that made me expect Stuart to kick him. Mrs. Kress held the pants in both hands. "What do I do with these, boys? There's no coat hanger to throw them on." Stuart stared at the shirt on the floor; he didn't say a word about the weight-lifting contest or even look up when Dwight yanked the comic book away.

"Louie Kress is a pantywaist," Aunt Peg said when I told her he'd yelled at his wife for wearing his old uniform. "It's no wonder Stuart is a little son of a bitch."

I thought about telling her what words Mr. Kress had used. If there was a word worse than pantywaist for a man, Aunt Peg would say it then. But I shut up, and Aunt Peg, holding up a *Time Magazine* from the week before, said, "Here's something more important than a baseball uniform." I looked at the pages she had opened to and saw "World's largest plane crash."

"One hundred and twenty-eight people dead," she said. "Two planes collided over the Grand Canyon. You wonder how that could happen with all that space up there." She tossed the magazine aside as if it were filled with nothing but monsters and victims. "Your father and mother would be interested in this story. They'd get a kick out of this, knowing what they know."

She looked like she was going to say more, but the phone rang, and it was Stuart. "One month from today," he said, picking a date so decisively I thought somebody had scheduled a second All-Star Game. "I'm calling Dwight next. One of you has something to prove." But his voice sounded like the school bus driver's when he threatened us that he wouldn't stop the next time we weren't all the way to the bus stop before he arrived. "OK," we'd promise, and be late again within a week because everybody knew he had to stop even if we were barely in sight.

Every afternoon, it was my job to walk down to where our mailbox was stuck among twelve others at the end of our street. "Rural free delivery," Aunt Peg would snort when I carried the mail into the house. "Anybody could steal whatever they want when it's way the hell down there."

The day after the All-Star Game I saw my sister and two boys smoking under the stand of wild cherry trees behind the mailboxes. "Pen-pal boy," my sister said when I opened the box to check inside. "Who'd you get a letter from today?"

I didn't look at the envelopes. "Nobody," I said.

"Jimmy Nobody. Joey Nobody. Some Mouseketeer? Write to Paul Anka," she said. "Tell him Diana lives here."

She'd bought Paul Anka's record the day it came out, acting like his begging Diana to wait for him was an omen. The boys laughed and dropped their butts, crushing them with their black, pointed shoes. "You know he's only sixteen," she said. "I'm going to be fifteen in September. If he wants Diana, he can have me right now."

One of the boys put his mouth close to her ear and whispered something that made her say, "You wish."

"Some wishes come true," he said aloud, but Diana took a step toward me and acted as if those boys had disappeared. "You know who writes to pen pals when they don't have to, don't you?" Diana said.

I thought she meant me. I had started writing a few months before the plane crash—I had letters from Cuffy, the boy on *Tales of the Foreign Legion*, and Rusty, from *Rin Tin Tin*.

"You don't know, do you?" Diana said. "That polio boy in my homeroom—he writes to everybody, that's who." She inhaled and blew the smoke out toward me. "Cripples write to pen pals. You don't have to be in a wheelchair."

I checked for cars and recrossed the road to our street. I was glad I'd never shown her my letter from Patience and Prudence, the singing sisters Aunt Peg thought were adorable. "That one is just your age," she said, whenever they were on television to sing "Tonight, You Belong to Me." "Is she Patience or Prudence?" And I was happy Diana was always in her room with the radio on when Aunt Peg told me every Saturday that I was born at the right time for the youngest Lennon sister when she made me watch Lawrence Welk with her.

The next Sunday, at our church, a man who I'd never seen before spoke about polio—how his daughter had gotten sick the day after she played in the sandbox he'd built for her. "I put that thing together," he said, "and that night I ripped it apart. I burned every board, and then I wheeled all that sand into the woods and dumped it."

For a while, I was paying attention, but it turned out his daughter had gotten polio four years ago, and he was only telling that story to show how he'd found his faith. He yammered on so long about God's will and trial-by-fire that I'd almost forgotten the polio girl until Aunt Peg, as soon as the service ended, said, "That man's crazy to think polio comes from sand."

I waited for Aunt Peg to say where it came from, but she didn't say anything about flies or filth or anything at all. Diana grinned at me. She leaned close and whispered, "You know why she won't say it? It's from not having sex. That's why kids get it."

It sounded so crazy it seemed like the truth. And then, when I was smart enough to remember that sometimes adults got it, she laughed. "It wears off," she said. "You have to keep doing it to stay safe."

I was going to summer camp that afternoon. I had a week of craft making, hiking, and swimming in Lake Worthy, where I wasn't allowed unless I proved I had a buddy.

"You keep your face out of that lake water," Aunt Peg said an hour later. "If there's polio at that camp, that's where it lives." We were waiting for my ride at the end of our driveway, and she pushed at two bricks that had worked loose. "Your father had a bad idea when he decided to make a driveway out of bricks," she said. "I'll have to pay to have these fixed every year." I wished that Lake Worthy had filled with silt. I wished there was a girl who wanted me to have her right now so we'd both be safe.

When I came home from summer camp, Aunt Peg told me Stuart had been sent to a camp of his own the day before. It lasted fifteen days. "Camp CrossRoads," Aunt Peg said. "Edie Kress says it shows boys how to take care of themselves."

"Stuart's already the strongest boy in our class," I said, but I was wondering why he hadn't said anything about going, whether you could sign up for a camp like that at the last minute.

Aunt Peg made that sound with her tongue. "No, not like that," she said, and then she made that sound again. "CrossRoads—as if somebody like Stuart Kress might make a right turn."

So for two weeks I spent my afternoons at Dwight Ware's house. Dwight seemed happy not to have Stuart around. "Him and his stupid weights," he said, but I didn't see him doing the Joe Bonomo routine. I was up to twice as many push-ups and pull-ups as when I'd started. I did pull-ups three times a day without worrying about Stuart walking outside to count my repetitions. I was going to be so ready for the weight-lifting test it didn't matter if Dwight was acting like he didn't care to keep me from knowing he stayed up past midnight to "pit one muscle against another" like the comic-book ad said.

What Dwight liked best was board games, and to tell the truth, when I played them with Dwight, I got almost as excited as he did because he was intense—Monopoly. Scrabble. Even Clue and Mr. Ree, the detective games that weren't much fun when there were only two players.

Even better, his mother didn't work like Aunt Peg and Mrs. Kress did. She kept us stuffed with snacks that looked like pictures—wagon wheels made from crackers, the spokes drawn with tiny pieces of rolled up cheese; cupcakes decorated to look like clown faces; cookies in the shapes of cars. She served real Coca-Cola, not the RC Aunt Peg bought because it was cheaper. And she watched television, the soap operas, though at 4:00 I always had to leave because she needed, she said, to get dinner ready for 5:30 when Mr. Ware walked in to sit down to a home-cooked meal.

Aunt Peg called Dwight's father "The Senator" because he kept his white shirt and tie on into the evening after work. He even cut his small lawn on Thursday nights still wearing that tie.

The lawn was so small he used a push mower, yet it took him only fifteen minutes to cut the grass, even walking slowly behind it in his wing tips. "Who does he think he's fooling?" Aunt Peg said. "He's the manager at the Sparkle Market."

Once, when I sat on the porch with Dwight while Stuart was at Camp CrossRoads, the two boys who had smoked with Diana at the mailboxes walked by. "There's Mr. Peepers," one of them said. I watched Mr. Ware, but he kept his stride behind the mower as if he didn't hear them, as if concentrating on the line of uncut grass made him deaf. It was a hand mower, though, so I knew he heard them when they both started yelling. "Mr. Peepers! Mr. Peepers!" They hollered as if he were their tenth grade English teacher, somebody to make fun of because he liked poems. I remembered Wally Cox and the Mr. Peepers character he played on television, and the first word that came to me was pantywaist.

"There's little Peepers," one of those boys finally said. Dwight had the same look as his father, staring at a point halfway down his asphalt driveway as if he'd suddenly noticed it was splitting.

"Who's your friend, little Peepers?" one shouted, and I decided to go home early. I saw Aunt Peg's car was gone when I walked up the street. Thursday was when she went to the movies with her friends. The living room was dark, and I didn't notice my sister and a boy I'd never seen before until I flipped on the dining-room light.

"What are you looking at?" my sister said.

"Nothing," I said, sounding like a pantywaist.

It was only his arm around her, and they were both sitting up, yet I knew I'd seen something else besides comfortable in my sister's expression. She wasn't relaxed. She wasn't happy. She was tense like boys on my Little League team, like she couldn't wait for something to happen yet was afraid, and in that moment I understood she had known that boy was going to move his hand from her shoulder to her breast if I hadn't walked in.

"Nothing is right," she said, and the boy stared at me until I felt myself turning as flabby as the shaped Jello molds Mrs. Ware served Dwight and me while we played Monopoly.

I waited for something to come to me, something clever to say, and then I squeaked, "OK."

Dwight kept track of statistics for every game we played during those two weeks. Who won. By how much. He even kept a record of how many times Miss Scarlet or Colonel Mustard was the killer.

By the time Stuart returned, Dwight was ahead in every game but Scrabble, but I was more worried that he would start babbling about those games in front of Stuart than I was about who'd won most often. Stuart looked stronger, no surprise, but he didn't talk about CrossRoads when he got back. "We're not allowed to tell," he said, his face so stern I just said "OK." He lifted every afternoon now, two different routines that he alternated. I decided I could wait until the "test day" for him to find out how little I could lift after a month of exercise. Besides, now that he lifted twice as much and twice as long each time, it was so boring at his house I'd play a board game at Dwight's before I'd stop in. Dwight didn't come at all.

Mr. Kress walked in late one afternoon just after I showed up near the end of Stuart's sets. "Lifting, huh?" he said, but Stuart didn't answer. He was doing arm curls, and for a moment I thought he'd say something when he let his right arm go slack and slipped the weight into his left hand.

Mr. Kress must have thought so, too, because he was smiling and watching until Stuart, without saying anything, brought the weight up to his chin with his left hand, inhaling. I shrugged, but that's all I could do because anybody could tell I wasn't lifting, sitting there in my white oxford and tie and gabardine pants because Aunt Peg was taking Diana and me out to eat at "a real restaurant."

Mr. Kress whistled then, and I couldn't tell if it was intentional or whether he'd just stuck at the beginning of a phrase like "Why don't you say something?", the air just rushing out without words. And then he turned and left.

Stuart didn't stop doing his curls, but suddenly I felt like I had to get out of there so I could rip off my tie and run to my room to change before I told Aunt Peg I wanted to go to the Brass Rail and have hamburgers and fries. I stopped by the door and waited until Stuart finished a set. "I have to go," I said. "Aunt Peg and her fancy restaurant, you know."

"Sure thing," Stuart said.

And then, because I wanted to say something besides lies, I said, "Your dad doesn't act the same since that baseball uniform thing."

Stuart picked up the curl bar, and for a moment I imagined him asking me to join him. "You're lucky," he said. "Your parents are perfect. They're dead."

I clenched my fists, but I didn't say anything. I heard Aunt Peg reminding me to "give people room," and I did. If I called him some obscene name now, I'd have to fight because of what I said. But if he kept going, adding something worse, I'd have to fight anyway, and it would be all I could do to keep Stuart from ripping my head off.

He let it go, starting another set even though I knew he wasn't ready, and on my way across our yards, I almost decided he was right, that what I thought about my parents was like the description in a story. They were like characters in a book I'd finished twenty-one months ago. Even if I read it again, nothing would be changed, so I'd never see what they did from any other point of view than an eleven-year-old boy's.

Once, a month before the plane crash, my father and I saw Mr. Kress take his belt to Stuart. My father, later, defended him. "It was wrong," he said, "but Stuart had it coming," and I stayed silent, understanding that my father meant for me to see that I was fortunate to have him for my father, someone who, even when his son had it coming, had the compassion not to deliver the punishment.

If only he hadn't told me this I would have simply hated Mr. Kress and added him to the list of people I was afraid of. Instead, I began to give him credit for carrying out his anger in front of us and questioned my father for using Mr. Kress's cruelty to make himself appear better.

"You have your father in you," Aunt Peg had said a hundred times since she'd moved in, and I knew she meant that as a caution. "Pearl said she liked sensitive in a man, but it's not far from sensitive to soft."

I thought about telling her the rest of that story about Mrs. Kress taking off that old baseball uniform after Mr. Kress called her a cunt. Just then, it seemed like an easy thing to do to become somebody in between a pantywaist and Mr. Kress.

During the second week in August, Diana stopped coming out of her room except for lunch and dinner, so when letters came from our school for both of us, Aunt Peg called her twice and then took a look at mine. It said polio shots were required. The school wanted to be sure nobody was missed, and therefore, starting the first week, I'd be getting mine unless I brought in proof from my family physician.

Aunt Peg called Diana once more and then opened her letter. I knew how it ended: "The shots will be free, so no student is denied protection because of his financial situation."

Aunt Peg made a phone call and then knocked on Diana's door. "Get dressed," she said. "I'm taking you to the doctor's."

Diana opened the door so quickly, I was sure she'd been listening on the other side. "I'm dressed," she said. "I'm ready."

"Good," Aunt Peg said, answering as if she wasn't surprised Diana was alive. She handed Diana her letter. "I won't have the two of you standing in line with white trash for a welfare vaccination."

Five minutes later we were headed toward the North Side instead of toward Doctor Brennan's. "We're going to my doctor, not that pantywaist your mother took you to. It's not that far. Doctor Jerabek was in World War II. He was a pilot. You can count on a man like that."

Doctor Jerabek's office was up a flight of stairs in a building with a discount clothing store on the street level. "This is new," Aunt Peg said. "This used to be a bridal shop. Your mother bought her wedding dress here."

The names were scraped off the door across the hall from Doctor Jerabek, but there was a light on and the sound of hammering. "That shyster lawyer must have retired or croaked," Aunt Peg said, and I saw Diana hug herself, shuddering as if the lawyer we didn't know was somehow related to us.

The shots were over and done with in five minutes. Aunt Peg wanted to make an appointment for our next shots, but Doctor Jerabek waved her off. "Don't worry yourself, Peg," he said. "Just give me a call when the time comes."

Aunt Peg smiled. She'd never married, and I thought she wished Doctor Jerabek, dark haired and thick muscled like a heavyweight boxer, meant her to call for herself. He walked us back through the waiting room where one old man was reading a *National Geographic.* "OK then," he said.

The old man put his magazine down, but Aunt Peg set herself between him and Doctor Jerabek. "Tell me," she said, "you were a pilot. How do two planes crash together in the air like they did awhile back?"

"The Grand Canyon thing?" Doctor Jerabek looked at Diana and then at me as if she'd asked him what happened to a plane when a bomb exploded inside it. "Somebody made a mistake."

"Yes, they did," Aunt Peg said, and then she nudged us through the door and herded us to the car.

When she made a left turn three blocks later, I knew she was taking us past her old apartment. "There it sits," she said, but neither Diana nor I had anything to add. We'd seen it before. We'd been inside the three rooms that looked out from the third floor onto a street of identical row houses. "Somebody else is enjoying the view now," she said.

I wanted to say that the neighborhood didn't look as dangerous as Aunt Peg had claimed. It just looked empty, as if everyone had moved. The whole time we drove along her old street we didn't see one person outside. "Good riddance," Aunt Peg said as we eased onto the main road. "And now the two of you are on a schedule. Doctor Jerabek wrote you a note. You can take it in to prove you don't have to stand in line with the likes of who lives back there."

That was the end of anybody saying anything for the six miles until we approached our street. "You reach out and get the mail," Aunt Peg said, pulling up beside the boxes.

Three boys were smoking under the cherry trees, the two I'd seen before and the boy who'd been on the couch with Diana. I wound down the window and opened the mailbox, but Diana jerked her head toward Aunt Peg.

"You know those boys?" Aunt Peg said, and Diana shook her head. "Good. You keep it that way."

One of the boys she'd smoked with pursed his lips into an exaggerated kiss. "Do they live on our street?" Aunt Peg said. "I've never seen them."

"No," Diana said, and then that boy make a circle with one finger and his thumb and poked a finger from his other hand through it. All of them laughed. "God help us," Aunt Peg murmured, turning up our street, and Diana opened the door before the car stopped moving, ran onto the porch, unlocked the door, and disappeared.

I stayed in the car for a minute after Aunt Peg got out. I knew Diana had gone to her room and closed the door, but from where I sat her room looked as empty as those houses in Aunt Peg's old neighborhood.

"It's about time," Stuart said when I told him I'd started my shots. "I thought when I came back from camp you'd be in an iron lung or something."

Dwight and I were in Stuart's basement passing around the September comic books, but then Stuart, as if he'd just remembered, said, "It's time for the weight-lifting contest. It's August 15."

"OK," I said, but Dwight didn't say anything, and I knew he hadn't been doing isometric-isotonics or even one push-up for the last month.

"Let's read these first. It's a good set," Dwight said.

"We can read them when you're done. Let's go."

"It's stupid. Who cares about lifting weights?"

"Who cares about comic books?" Stuart threw the one he was holding against the wall. When it smacked against the floor, I saw that the staples had come loose, separating the cover from the inside pages.

Dwight crawled over to it and pushed the cover back on. "You're the all-time queer," Stuart said. "Go read your comic books to your mother."

"At least my mother isn't a cunt," Dwight yelled, and then he sprinted up the stairs and out the back door, the screen door slamming behind him. Stuart went up two at a time and ran after him, so by the time I got outside, they were tangled on the other side of the yard, over by where our property began.

Stuart hugged Dwight down to the ground right beside where the ants Aunt Peg had swept had rebuilt. "You fairy," Stuart said, but Dwight barely struggled.

Stuart wrestled Dwight sideways, pushing his face into the ants. That was it, I thought, Dwight with a face full of ants and me not having to do anything but act like I could outlift him.

Somehow, though, Dwight panicked so much from the ants that he managed to roll over, and Stuart lost his balance just enough for Dwight to heave himself up and run as far as the end of our driveway before Stuart tackled him again.

Stuart put him in a headlock, swinging one knee like a fist into Dwight's stomach. "I give," Dwight screamed. "I give."

Stuart twisted Dwight's head one more time. "I could kill you," he said, but he let go and Dwight scrabbled up to his hands and knees, his eyes streaming and snot running from his nose, his hands scratching like a dog's paws until he happened on to one of the loose bricks at the end of our driveway.

Just as Stuart sat down on the grass, Dwight swung around and smacked the side of his head with the brick. Stuart said "Unhhh" and slumped, his head banging once on the driveway. He didn't move. "And now you're dead," Dwight yelled, starting to run down the street toward his house, the brick falling from his hand right before he reached his yard.

I heard Diana shouting from our porch. "Peepers did it. Peepers killed him." But I kept staring at that brick lying in the street three houses away. It wasn't until Aunt Peg stood over me, saying, "Get in the house," that I looked at Stuart and saw that he still hadn't moved.

An ambulance came. From my room I couldn't tell how Stuart was doing, but after the ambulance pulled away, its siren turned on, Diana shouted, "Now you're in for it" through my closed door and stomped away without waiting for an answer. I sat on my bed staring at the carpet, moving my head from side to side to make the pattern shift from whirlpools to open mouths to circled fingers. I heard voices and doors slamming, but I kept that pattern changing, and then I remembered the three-in-one Winky picture my father had of Jesus on the cross, his eyes closed, his eyes open, his eyes looking up to heaven, and I started trying to work out the sequence for those eyes, which face of Jesus came first.

I was still staring, minutes later, when Aunt Peg swung open my door and walked in. She'd promised, on my twelfth birthday, not to enter my room unless she knocked and I said it was OK. She hadn't broken that promise for ten months, but there she was beside me, gesturing with the short, choppy wave she used when she was angry, like she was sweeping crumbs off a countertop, and I couldn't make my mouth move to complain.

"Get out here," she said, and when I turned the corner into the hall I saw the fat policeman in our living room. "You tell the truth now," my aunt said. "Don't you lie to save your friend."

I thought my friend was dead, but then I realized she meant

Dwight. I wanted to tell Aunt Peg that just because we played to-gether didn't mean we were friends. It was because we lived three houses apart. It was because Dwight always had Coke and potato chips and candy bars.

"A likely fractured skull," the policeman said. "You need to be a man about this, young fellow."

I wanted to walk to the window and check to see if there was a police car outside of Dwight's house, but I sat down on the couch and waited. "The boy may not recover, if you know what I mean," he said to Aunt Peg, and she nodded like I did when I was listening to Mr. Gorman, my social studies teacher, listing the succession of British kings and queens.

"He'll tell the truth," Aunt Peg said, and when I started my story, I said Dwight was being beaten and grabbed the brick and swung to save himself. I said he didn't try to hit anybody in the head, that's just where it landed. That Stuart was bigger and stronger and was choking him, and if the fight had gone on another minute I thought I was going to have to jump in to save Dwight from strangling.

I didn't even think about what Dwight might say to a policeman. For all I knew, he'd confess, say he wanted to kill Stuart and was sorry he was still alive. Dwight, I thought, knew I disliked him and wouldn't expect me to do anything but make sure I was in the clear.

So it made me feel good to lie like that, making Dwight look bet-ter. I felt like I was a hero almost, filling in details about Stuart kick-ing Dwight, Stuart choking him and calling him names.

"What names?" the policeman said.

"Fairy," I said. When all the policeman did was nod, I added "Queer," and when the policeman kept his pencil poised, I said "Cunt," and Aunt Peg had her hand to her mouth so quickly I knew those words sounded like I'd said them a thousand times before. A second later I heard Diana's door slam, so I knew she'd heard every word.

Right then I didn't care. I wasn't saying those words. I was quoting them. And Stuart Kress was the kind of boy who would say them if he'd had to—if he was losing a fight or things were even—that's what he would yell—I knew it. So nothing I said was a lie.

"Well," the policeman said. He was sweating, his shirt stained where the folds of his stomach creased. When he stood up, the dark lines ran under his arms. "You ought to be keeping an eye on this one," he said to Aunt Peg. "There's work to be done."

Aunt Peg didn't say anything. She didn't nod or change expression. She didn't move toward the door as the policeman left, didn't acknowledge him as he opened it.

"OK, Jason," Aunt Peg said then, "he's done here, that's for sure." The policeman hesitated in the doorway, and Aunt Peg put her hands on my shoulders as if he were gone and began to work her fingers into where the shoulders sloped up into my neck. "You remember how your father always laughed at that clown with the sad face? What's his name?"

I waited for the door to close before I said, "Emmett Kelly," but I wanted her to keep going, tell the rest of the story so I'd get it straight instead of imagining the details. Her hands were like a man's. I thought she could rip my head off right then, just lift and tear like a werewolf or a giant mantis. "I knew you'd know his name," she said. "You remember all those little things."

I heard the policeman's car door slam, and when the engine turned over, Aunt Peg let her hands fall to her sides, but neither of us moved.

"That fat pantywaist," she said, and then she stopped as if she'd just been clearing her throat instead of starting a sentence.

"What?" I finally said. I was sure she was going to say he was like my father, that he had a clown's sadness, the kind that nobody took seriously. And when she didn't answer, she started to look older, stooped, like she would be in a Winky that shifted you into an old person, somebody who was a pantywaist now no matter how strong he'd been.

"Never you mind," she said, but it was too late. She turned back into Aunt Peg, but I'd seen what she was becoming.

"Sit yourself down for a minute," she said, and she opened a cabinet and pulled out a stack of my parents' old records. "Let's give these a listen."

I sat on the edge of the couch and waited, and when the song began, I recognized it as one my mother had bought just before the plane crash—"Only You" by the Platters.

Aunt Peg sang along, holding another record, so I knew to keep sitting. The records were 78s. At the store the shelves were full of mostly 45s now, and the records Aunt Peg had stacked looked like they had been recorded before I was born.

"Do you know what your mother's favorite song was when they went off on that trip?" she asked.

She lifted off the Platters and slid the next record into place over the small knob, placing the needle into the rim of the spinning record. "Here it is," she said. "Listen." I knew this song, too—"Cry Me a River."

"Come on and dance with your Aunt Peg," she said.

Any other time I would have said "No" and backed out of the room, but I thought I owed it to her. Right now I was sure that policeman was asking Dwight how he came to smashing Stuart's head.

"Do you know who's singing?" she said, letting me lead.

"Julie London."

"All the little things," she said. "You're a natural. You'll be a heart-breaker someday."

I wasn't sure she meant my remembering names or my dancing, but I shuffled back and forth, my arms extended, afraid that Aunt Peg might pull me in close when Julie London sang, "I cried a river over you" in that smoky voice my mother tried to imitate when she sang along.

"Your father never danced. Your poor mother had to sit it out or wait for a peppy tune so she could hotfoot it with a girlfriend."

Just then I wanted to ask Aunt Peg whether or not you'd have time to say anything in a plane when a bomb went off, but she had her eyes closed, swaying, her feet stopped, and I stood still, letting her guide my arms back and forth until the song ended. "Oh," she said then, "you'll be something," and I decided that a bomb in a plane would just rip everybody apart, that nothing would be said by any-body except what was already coming out of their mouths the sec-ond before they exploded.

Book Owner

After I had my tonsils removed, my mother bought a ream of ruled paper and drew columns on fifty sheets. "This will get you started," she said. "You can print all the numbers as high as you want and see how you feel about going on when you finish."

I started in at once. Nobody had ever done this, I thought, reaching one thousand, two thousand, three thousand, and ready to fill more pages the following day.

"No mistakes," my mother said, proofreading before I fell asleep. "You haven't got one of those numbers wrong or out of place."

I was six years old. The next morning my aunt brought me a game of Cootie, and I took turns for four players at once, rolling the die for each of them, not counting past six for three hours.

* * *

On the first day of school, in third grade, Miss Ozminski told us it was time to master cursive, and she was going to start us with ovals repeated across the first page of our writing notebooks. She had filled our inkwells while we were outside for afternoon recess, and now we needed to slip the steel point she was passing out into the wooden stick that was coming around next.

We held our new pens up to show her we were ready to write. Dip and swirl, she explained, and don't let the tip rest on the paper. "Around, around, around," she chanted. "Stay inside two lines." We had to master the Peterson method unless we wanted to be babies like the second graders who printed with pencils. We had to be careful or we'd be inkwell spillers, the stained ones who were going to be failures, heading straight for the welfare line where the worthless went since the Democrats had started the handout system.

All year we had blotters from the bank, the previous month stamped on each one as they were passed back the row. When March was handed out during the first week in April, a comic wind trying to blow open a secure vault, Miss Ozminski told us we had to use cursive for every assignment or we wouldn't get credit.

We wrote a letter to our parents, signing our names. We wrote a letter to the bank president to thank him for the blotters, signing our names. My signature was perfect. I could write it the same way over and over. I'd signed it where it said BOOK OWNER on the inside covers of the multiple copies of the history book we'd finished in January and put away on a shelf in the back of the room. George Vaughn, I wrote, knowing nobody would see my name until next September. George Vaughn. Every boy and girl would think I'd read the book they had. I imagined my letters arriving. I imagined the next ones I would write. I wanted every letter of my name to be legible, thirty-five third graders in September 1957 seeing how George Vaughn, a boy they all knew, had mastered penmanship.

* * *

At the beginning of fourth grade, Miss Logue assigned us pen pals. "Miss Ozminski tells me you all had perfect penmanship when school was dismissed in June," she said. "We shall see. Now you have to write to someone you have never met. The first impression that someone will have of you is through your handwriting."

All of the addresses were in Canada because, she said, the students were certain to be strangers. Pamela Phelan waved her hand to claim she already wrote to famous people. She'd received, just last week, a letter from Tommy Sands, who told her he was glad she loved his song "Teenage Crush." She had a letter signed by Timmy, who was saved each Sunday by dependable Lassie. "The best one," she said, "is from Winston Churchill," but nobody in the room was impressed by a letter from someone older than our grandparents.

"None of them," Miss Logue said, "live in Canada," and I wrote and wrote until I had three pages to send to Bradley Lester, who lived in Halifax.

I thought everybody would get an A for friendly letters, but Ronald Riggs went above and under the lines, and Don Gebert spelled seventeen words wrong and forgot his return address.

On television that week, Lassie ran home to bark Timmy's mother to the cave where Timmy was trapped. Lassie pawed at the rocks as if she could help open a space. She crawled inside when a hole opened and stayed with Timmy until men arrived to clear the old mine. Because Pamela Phelan had used the school address the next time she wrote to the stars, the school secretary delivered another letter to her from Timmy during geography. It was typed and said he was happy she loved his dog and that he had signed a picture of Lassie for her. There was nothing else in the envelope, and Pamela thought the secretary had steamed it open and stolen the picture for her daughter.

The next day a letter came for Audrey Weeks, who'd written her own name and address twice on the white envelope, getting it back as if she'd answered herself.

* * *

By now Mussolini is just a name. He played second fiddle to Hitler, and so nobody can quite remember what he was doing during the war. But in November, right after I got my second letter from Bradley Lester, who printed, Miss Logue told us about a woman and her daughter who had just discovered thirty volumes of Mussolini's diaries, something so special people wanted to buy them. "Of course," Miss Logue said, "you have to make sure he actually wrote them."

Pamela Phelan waved her hand until Miss Logue called on her. "Who would know if the words were his?" she asked.

Miss Logue smiled like she'd stolen that picture of Lassie herself. "Mussolini had a son," she said. "He says they are genuine."

Pamela Phelan waved her hand again. "Maybe," she said, "he's in on it, helping those women fake the diaries for the money."

I thought Miss Logue would be angry, but she pulled down the map of Europe to show us where Italy was. "The diaries have been tested by history and handwriting experts," she said, "men who are professors at famous universities." She pointed at Rome as if we were supposed to imagine the Mussolini diaries lined up on a bookshelf there. "You know what one of those experts said?" she went on. "'Thirty volumes of manuscript cannot be the work of a forger, but of a genius.'"

* * *

"You believe in the ten commandments, don't you, George?" my mother asked when I started fifth grade, meaning for me to say the handwriting was God's just like the fortune scripted on Belshazzar's wall. If God can write from heaven, she reasoned, so can the saved.

She started telling me the story of Baron DeGuldenstubbe, who supplied paper to the dead by laying it beside their tombs and statues. He expected autographs from the afterlife, and his faith, he said, had been rewarded when they wrote short notes to him, signing their names.

My mother said Plato wrote in Greek, Virgil in Latin, Mary Stuart in English. Altogether, she said, the Baron received five hundred letters sent to him in twenty different languages.

"Sure," I said.

"Well," she said, "let's see then." And she locked paper and a pen in a silver-plated box one Sunday morning, keeping me quiet for one hour because any sound at all would frighten off the dead. I measured the minutes, listening and listening for the faint scratches of ghostwriting.

And there, when my mother lifted the lid, were three phrases on the paper: *Be Good. Obey. Believe the Bible.*

That box sat three feet below her living room cross, Christ close enough, she said, to have written that advice I'd take or suffer punishment, selecting English from the infinite languages in which he could write warnings for boys.

The next day Pamela Phelan told me the Mussolini diaries had unraveled. The woman had spent a lot of time perfecting Mussolini's handwriting, so it had taken awhile for somebody with sense to catch her.

Pamela Phelan wanted me to go with her when she told Miss Logue, but I shook my head. All I could think about was how long it would take to handwrite thirty volumes. What patience she had. How good she was at forgery.

*   *   *

In seventh grade, I copied a story for school. I stole it from a collection of horror stories in a paperback that cost fifteen cents used. I was sure Miss Buchanowski wouldn't recognize it because she would never read a book with a picture of a woman being strangled on the cover. She gave me an A. And anyway, I hadn't copied it entirely. I made sure it was a man who was strangled. I had a woman do the killing. It was easy. All I did was reverse the names from beginning to end and make sure I didn't slip up and have the wrong descriptions with the switched names. "Do you think a woman would be strong enough to do this?" Miss Buchanowski wrote underneath the A she printed at the end.

A week later, my mother told me she could write everything I said, no matter how fast I said it. "That's impossible," I said, "but I don't know what to say."

"Tell me that story you wrote," she said. "Say it as fast as you can."

She smiled as my sentences sped into a stutter of phrases so stupid I sounded like an idiot when she read all of them exactly back to me from shorthand. In her notebook was nothing but the curves and squiggles of crib-art, and when, angry at myself for giving her such easy words, I speed-read each verse of the longest Psalm, she recited those scribbles as if she were cued by the whispered voice of God.

Afterward, my mother told me about a man named Hendrik

Hertzberg, who produced a book called *One Million*. Each chapter consisted entirely of dots in varying numbers.

* * *

When I was a freshman in college, a man jostled his bar stool closer and told me, as soon as I turned, he could tell my fortune. I said, "Sure thing," and started picking pages from the fresh issue of *Life* he'd laid on the bar. "This here magazine is as infallible as the Bible," he said. "You choose four pages that don't have any ads on them, and the numbers will tell you your future job, your wife's name, how many children you'll have, and the city where you'll live the longest."

Why not? I wasn't reading anymore. I was watching my life-to-be on the television news, waiting for a pizza and a beer and June to come so I could enlist. I was ready, in 1967, to end all that Commie bullshit. I fluttered the pages: "Salesman," he said. "Sarah. None. Cleveland."

When I said "thanks" instead of buying him a beer for his trouble, he insisted me back to *Life* to choose one more page that would tell me the number of the year I'd die. What the hell, I thought, and flipped to the next page with no ads. He looked at me so long I swallowed my draft in one gulp, and then he smiled and clapped me on the back, laughing at the lifeline he'd counted for me, the two of us laughing then, though I didn't believe anything that prophet was saying.

* * *

My mother cleaned up crime with food that next summer—bacon and eggs, toast, grapefruit sections she carved out while I showered the dry heaves away like sin. "You eat your breakfast," she said, and I managed, one slow mouthful at a time, wiping the grease and soft yolk with bread until I could see my face in that spotless plate. Not yet 6 A.M., but it was the time I drove into Pittsburgh for the first shift at Heinz.

In the middle of June, I stole the letter to my parents from the registrar, who quantified one mess I'd made. I had a semester to clean up my grades if nobody knew I'd failed. I changed the F I'd received in calculus to a B and recalculated my quality points; I changed the D for French to a B- and tallied again, getting myself to 2.33, all the cheating I was inclined to do. I scribbled all over that sheet of paper as if adding up the quality points was so important I had to do it three times. My mother said, "You try harder next year." My father shook his head, but he believed I was making a sacrifice when, in July, I signed on for Vietnam, rid of college and Heinz with one signature.

"Just don't you make a mess of yourself," my father said. "You don't come crying to me if you don't measure up."

My mother said, "You come home in one piece."

*   *   *

The first morning in Vietnam, a captain looked all of us cherries over like he was evaluating girls standing along a wall in the gym at a high school dance. He motioned me forward and took me aside while the others waited. "You a college boy?" he said.

"Not exactly," I said.

"That's a *yes*. You don't have to be coy with me, son. I can see it all over you."

"I left after a year, sir."

"You can spell, right? You know what a comma is, correct?"

"Sure."

He changed my orders. I sat in Saigon at a desk typing forms and memos and letters. I described three battles in letters I sent home. I never said I was in them, though I included as much detail as I could from the stories I heard in bars. "I'm still in one piece," I would say at the end of each letter.

"I pray for your safety," my mother repeated before she ended each of hers. "Your father is proud."

"I was lucky," I said to everyone who asked when I came home, and let others decide what that meant. Businesses in my town were hiring veterans. I started selling Chevrolets. *American through and through*, the sign on the window said. When customers found out I was just back from a combat tour, they shook my hand and trusted my offers. It wasn't me telling them war stories, but I was good for business. Consensus said I was a stoic. How quiet I was about the war was like a good mystery.

The second month back I read about how the women who'd forged the Mussolini diaries had resurfaced. Those diaries, they said, were authentic. Their confessions had been coerced. Everybody knows what happens when the police get hold of you, they said. We're not responsible for what we say under such pressure. They were giving an interview because they'd sold $71,400 worth of diary pages to the *Sunday Times of London*.

* * *

A woman who lived just fifty miles away couldn't stop writing. Her story was on television, followed by the news of history's famous cases, people who wrote word after word, sentence after sentence, until they had pages and pages and pages.

For privacy, she said, she built a room. That's where she stored her notebooks, the announcer said, like William Harvey, who dug secret spaces under his house in which to think, discovering, meanwhile, the functions of the heart and the circulation of blood.

The announcer looked into the camera as if he were checking to see I was paying attention. "There's more," he said. "When he wrote in those caves he dug for himself, Harvey spelled *pig* with three gs, tripled the last letters of *heart* and *blood*, a kind of shorthand, experts explain, for his nonstop writing." Perhaps, I thought, listening, Harvey kept writing the same letter because he was holding his breath with his pen hand to hear better his heart.

The woman who claimed she was writing the serial book of her life brought a book to the camera. Months, she said, it's taken, to work a week into the long story of the difficult act of art. "Look here," she murmured, opening the volume, and the reporter softly read: "I began to write. I kept writing. The light changes, I write. I write. I write. I write." Sounding out a pulse, the words swirled, then reswirled, like blood.

I looked up compulsive writing at the library and read the story of a man named Robert Shields, who recorded his life in a diary divided into five-minute intervals. He was so obsessed with getting the maximum number of chapters that sleep became an anxiety. He woke to the joy of "I rose and reached for my pen." He worked the minutes into shape until twenty-four years had inched into twenty-one boxes full of five-minute diaries. When he brushed his teeth, he detailed it; while he shaved, he wrote. Everything he ate was recorded in the lines of the last few minutes.

Some mornings Robert Shields made a resolution to quit. Write, he said to himself: *This is the last line*, and then he recorded the next secrets—breakfast, the shades of light in the kitchen, how many steps he took leaving and returning to the room where the diary offered itself like pornography. Until 11:20—settling into bed, pulling up the blankets. 11:25—turning off the lights, writing in the dark. 11:30—writing, still writing, still writing.

* * *

Eighteen months later I was in the newspaper, a picture of me with my wallet, its papers and cards fanned across a desk in front of me. "Stolen," I'm quoted as saying, "at the physical I took for Vietnam."

The old pictures look like they are arranged for a séance, calling up the ghosts from the black and white of nearly four years before, their faces lost in the attic of a thief, in a locked black box, perhaps, kept with a thousand other stolen wallets. The pay rate on my wage stub seemed like slavery; the woman whose signature was on a creased receipt was dead. The college student I was in the picture the newspaper had reprinted was looking at the camera like the treed bear in the photograph placed below it on the third page of the second section. "Hunger," the article about it said, "drew it here, too close to town." The bear stared at the people-rings that spread from its tree as if the oak were quivering in water, as if that water, bewildered, rippled endlessly, unknowable as reasons for returning a wallet, believing in an address four years after theft, that someone would forward it, that George Vaughn would open it, amazed, and whisper, "Jesus, Son of Mary, this is mine."

* * *

"You're not there," my mother said one afternoon the following week. She explained that she meant parts of me—one eye, a button on my shirt, two fingers on one hand—holes in me wherever she looked.

To change the missing things, she turned her head, choosing her losses, retrieving the pieces of me she thought were lost.

The doctor said migraines. When they persisted, another diagnosed socoma, blind spots that open, then never close, my mother staring and staring, finally, so she could learn to complete things by imagining what was lost. She worked out shapes, completing squares and circles and lines. And then she forgot my name, staring and staring and completing nothing about the shape and sound of the word.

* * *

I carried trivia books to work with me and kept them handy for the slow hours. *The 1886 Appleton's Cyclopedia of American Biography contained eighty-four phony biographies submitted by an unknown correspondent. For several editions, some of those entries stayed. It took until 1936 to weed out the final fraud.* That's what I was reading when a woman my age dropped into the chair across from my desk so suddenly, without saying a word, that I slammed it shut like it was full of naked women.

"So," she said, leaning forward, taking my eyes right down to the cleavage she was showing. "You're the hero George Vaughn." She sat up straight, her nipples showing against her low-cut cotton top. "When I heard your name at the five-year reunion," she went on, "I said, 'Roseanne Moore, you look that boy up in your yearbook.' But I'm here to tell you I was worried because I thought you were somebody else. He turned out to be Richard Schneider. Were you friends with him?"

"No," I said, and Roseanne Moore looked confused.

"Well, I was glad you weren't Richard Schneider," she said. "Why didn't you come to the reunion?"

I shrugged, coming up with nothing whatsoever I could say. Roseanne Moore reached across my desk, laying her hands on mine, and smiled. "Oh, I know how it is," she said. "After all, we're not in high school anymore, are we?"

We had six weeks of sex, but Roseanne Moore was fond of going to places where people who recognized me were drinking enough to make them ask for war stories. I started cooking in for us, filling the refrigerator with beer and wine so it was easy to suggest staying in my apartment.

At the beginning of the seventh week, Roseanne looked at me as I handed her a glass of wine in my kitchen. "Everything about you is perfect," she said, "but there's not enough 'everything.'"

She held my eyes, waiting until I said, "What does that mean?"

"I admire you, but I don't love you." She smiled. "That's it," she said. "It's like I've been learning something, and now I'm graduating."

* * *

While Roseanne was finishing her homework, Clifford Irving deceived five hundred handwriting experts hired by his book publisher to insure against the embarrassment of publishing a forgery. All of them agreed it was the genuine Howard Hughes who wrote the supporting documents to verify the authenticity of the interviews for the forthcoming biography. For Irving to forge such an amount of material "would be beyond human ability," said one expert.

I moved to a small city three hours' drive from where I'd grown up. My first day at work two customers mentioned my military service, hinted at their desire to hear me recount my heroism. "I was lucky," I said to both of them, and they nodded like they'd heard the Pope.

After they left, I opened my newest book to the story of Marva

Drew, who had set out to record all the numbers from one to one million, in pica type. She'd started in 1968, while I was in Vietnam, and now she was almost done. There was a picture of her sitting at her typewriter, fingers poised. The caption read "Marva Drew types 925,458." She was on page 2,329, all of the other 2,328 pages stacked in one pile like a novel manuscript beside the typewriter. Though we hadn't spoken since I'd moved, I wanted to call my mother to tell her this, to see if she would encourage me to take up where I left off once, to sit down to break Marva Drew's record.

For a week I intended to call, and when so much time went by, I thought, while I wrote up bills of sales for strangers as if they were prescriptions for happiness, about driving back to visit. That people read promises into my words seemed dreadful. That I could be admired without earning it sickened me.

Five months later, on the last afternoon of her life, my mother, living 140 miles away, mailed me the first letter she'd sent since I'd moved. My father called me with the news the following evening. "I didn't want to bother you," he said. "There's time enough for you to make the funeral by driving in the morning, and you won't have to fend off all those people who want to hear you talk about the war instead of your mother."

Just before I left, the mailman brought the letter. "I'm so proud of you," she wrote. "The story of your life is adding up to something."

Her penmanship was perfect. Every letter was formed so clearly there was no mistaking what she said. "Here's one for you," she wrote. "In 1738, a man named Hermann Boerhaave died and left behind one copy of a self-published, sealed book entitled *The Onliest and Deepest Secrets of the Medical Art*. The book sold for twenty thousand dollars at auction, and when the new owner opened it, everything but the title page was blank."

The stationery lay warm in my hands; it seemed to yellow and curl from the air I was drawing toward me. Her signature was a beautiful Sharon; my address in Maryland was scripted so carefully it looked as if it had been written by machine.

I could have taken three days off. There was a death-in-the-immediate-family benefit in my contract. I hadn't missed one minute in the 142 working days since I'd started. I was twenty-five years old and counting.

Pharisees

Jim Grayson taught good and evil. He had his students research the Catholic hierarchies to learn what the saints and the devils accounted for in this world that was going to hell now or even sooner.

Once upon a time, he explained to his classes, the saints managed our bodies. St. Blaise commanded the throat. St. Lucy was in charge of the eyes. "And St. Erasmus?" he asked them. And when every hand in his room stayed down, he said triumphantly, "The guts."

Jim Grayson passed out pictures of all those saints in September. Whoever fell into your hands was who you reported on. A thousand words. With footnotes and a bibliography. Investigate, he said. Proceed.

When anyone complained because this was a public school, he said his class was World Cultures. Isn't Christianity important?

When somebody said he was teaching Catholicism, Grayson said he always mentioned the other religions by way of comparison. "I could give them the Greeks and the Romans," Grayson said, "but that would be a waste. You don't need to know them; you just remember the names so the allusions come to you."

"We start with the saints," Grayson told me during my first month on the job, "because belief and values are the beginning of everything. And we do the devils because they follow the saints like dogs." He paused, waiting, I imagined, for whatever sign I would give that signaled disapproval. "And then we move on," he added. "We do politics and art. We do the myths." And they did, even opening, from time to time, the textbook approved by the school board. But what made those saints and devils part of history's curriculum was that Jim Grayson got results, every last one of his students for the first five years he'd taught in that room passing the January and June state-mandated standardized tests. If he pulled off that feat this year, Grayson would have nearly a thousand students take those tests without failing. I knew all this because the principal had told me, my first day, that the only thing he hoped for me as a teacher of American history was that being close to Jim Grayson would rub some of his test-results magic off on me.

In October, Jim Grayson concentrated on the devils. Beelzebub, who took advantage of our pride; Astaroth, who preyed on sloth. Those were the only two I'd ever heard of before Grayson handed me a copy of his instructions for the next thousand-word report. Gressil. Asmodeus. Verrine. He had them in some sort of order. I couldn't even remember the one that was supposed to be inside Regan in *The Exorcist*. I thought one of those names might set me off to giving it credit for the head-turning and the crucifix masturbation, but if Grayson mentioned it, I didn't recognize the evil.

Hardly anyone complained. I found out fast enough that it was the fundamentalists who sent anonymous letters to the superintendent of schools because a book contained the word *damn* or suggested sex could be something you did for fun.

As soon as I Xeroxed a story to supplement my "American Culture" unit, I had a problem with a parent because of the word *prostitute*, not to mention *whore*. Jim Grayson thought I should pay more attention to the stories I chose. "Preview," he said. "It's the only way to beat the devil."

I wanted to tell him I'd read that story in high school, but instead I said, "I thought there was a whole platoon of devils I have to beat."

"You have help," he said. "You have Muriel."

For a moment I thought he was confusing me with another teacher who'd tossed skepticism his way. Somebody with a wife named Muriel. Somebody old because I hadn't met anyone under the age of seventy with that name. "Your birthday's July ninth, isn't it?" he asked.

I nodded. Here was coincidence, the soon-to-be-retiree on our staff with the same date of birth as mine. "Everyone has an angel assigned to them on the day they're born. Yours is Muriel."

Grayson kept the straightest face I could imagine this side of the grave. And then, I'll admit, I thought, *As long as this guy teaches here I'll never be the worst fool in the school.*

It was the year of the swine flu scare, Gerald Ford declaring every good citizen needed to be inoculated before Christmas or the country would go the epidemic way of 1918.

When I brought it up in November, the mass vaccinations already begun, Jim Grayson disagreed. "You don't need inoculation," he said. "You need prayer."

I told him I'd prayed for five years, from age seven to twelve, for God to make my eyes better again. Those were the words I'd used every night. "God, please make my eyes better again." My mother had suggested them. "Give God time," she'd said. "He's testing you."

My prescription changed three times, and when I started eighth grade I began to pray for contact lenses so I could see better and not look like a geek to girls.

"You need to research," Grayson said. "Eyes have a history with saints."

I wished I'd kept science to myself. I wished him one of those ancient self-declared doctors who sniffed urine and drew blood before they walked to the next house, leaving prayer as an antidote to their diagnosis. Every month, after his classes received their next ancient name, his students had a week to research and turn in a copy of their notes. They had a weekend to outline and turn in a copy of that. And then a week to write a thousand words, penmanship affecting the grade. "It's discipline," Grayson said, and then he looked me in the eye as if he had known me long enough to confide a secret and added, "You should try it."

I'd heard the rest of his lesson plan before. A report, Jim Grayson wrote on his syllabus, was a personal letter to the world. What we researched and wrote was our signature, revealed what was in our hearts. I'd made a copy of one a student had shown me, so I knew what he had in mind. Before I could stop myself, I'd sat down and read all the way through to the part where he spoke of the wonders earned by checking margins. How half an inch was half an inch and nothing else. I stuffed it into a drawer in my desk before I started to read it twice and maybe began to say those things in class.

Grayson assigned the saints of medicine in November, though it seemed to me that they weren't very comforting. St. Roche, students told me, brought the plague. St. Anthony was in charge of infection. "St. Anthony's fire?" my wife, Sarah, had asked when I brought home that news the week before, and I shook my head like I was learning the intricacies of foreign cultures. I kept the rest to myself, how St. Lawrence brought the backache and St. Dympna was the one who brought misery to the brain. The saints, it seemed, were almost as bad as the devils, and they didn't offer any pleasure in return for their consequences, and then Sarah, to my surprise, said, "How about St. Vitus? Isn't he the one who teaches us the dance of tics and shivers?"

Sarah slid into the middle of the kitchen. She twitched a little. She shuffled in place. She jerked one arm and then the other, still shuffling. "My mother used to say I had the St. Vitus Dance when I was little," she said. "Invite this guy out for a beer. If he says 'yes,' I want to come, too."

Loitering in the hall outside his door, I listened to Grayson one afternoon. "We need to know," Grayson said, "the ways we can fail, the fates of the dead. Remember the devils. Remember the ways they want your bodies. Remember their names, the sound of sin."

I moved a step farther from the door, beginning to believe one of the saints would lift Grayson's ears like a dog's so he could sense me lurking. When his voice rose, I thought he might be approaching the door on the practiced feet of a wilderness scout.

"Recite temptations," he said. "Recite desire. Belberith, Astoroth—repeat them, repeat them," Grayson tolled.

Rosier, Verrier, Carnivean. Apparently, he was beginning the second level of devils, a list, from top to bottom, of names I'd never heard. I bent over the fountain and let the water splash against my closed mouth until I was ready to stride past his door as if I were walking somewhere.

That evening, I heeded the call of Gerald Ford, choosing the prudence of a vaccine rather than the mortal danger of trusting in the saint of swine flu, somebody who might not know the virus had mutated into a thing so deadly an angel couldn't prevent it. "OK," I had said to Sarah after several delays. "OK." We rushed to the clinic, beating the posted closing time by three minutes. The room was empty except for volunteers who chattered among themselves while we filled out forms and agreed not to sue the United States if we were one of the rarities who suffered adverse side effects. Those volunteers packed up and reached for their coats while we received our shots. I took a couple of steps, looked back at the puzzled nurse, and managed to squeak, "I think I'm in trouble here," cursing Jim Grayson for calling this one correctly before I tumbled at the feet of my wife and a group of good-hearted strangers.

In the first few seconds of recovery, I was surrounded, lifted to my feet, and helped, with all deliberate speed, behind a curtain. The cot they laid me on wasn't a precaution; neither was the curtain. It was a makeshift office for the volunteer staff, some of whom might have wished to stretch out for a few minutes during their twelve-hour shift.

Those doctors and nurses in that New York clinic knew the same thing as I did—a couple of days earlier, in Pittsburgh, some people had died. Hovering over me, they weren't smiling, and I didn't blame them a bit. Neither I nor Sarah could manage anything but the patient silence of the pulled-aside at a customs checkpoint until they decided I'd fainted because I hadn't eaten anything but a bowl of cereal ten hours before the shot. I celebrated by drinking two cartons of orange juice, and then Sarah and I ate cheeseburgers that we both knew had been delivered for the staff to eat.

"Inoculation is the devil's work," Grayson said, making Sarah's evening in five words. I could tell she was happy to be having a beer with our town's personification of lunacy.

"I'm a disciple of Gerald Ford," I said. "It was a kind of Last Supper with a happy ending."

"I don't understand," Grayson said. "The Last Supper had a happy ending. We're all saved now if we believe."

"I prefer a resurrection in the here and now. I was pleased as can be to wake up on earth."

Jim Grayson cupped his beer with both hands in a way that made me believe he was trying to appear thoughtful and profound. When he looked into the frosted mug, I wanted to crucify him right then and there, nail that Christ-poser's hands to the wall and slosh that beer all over him, telling him to extend his tongue like a frog if he wanted to lick any of it as it dripped to the linoleum floor.

"I hate these frozen mugs," Grayson said instead. "All the condensation ice slides into the beer and waters it down."

Sarah said, "You got that right," which made me have to argue.

"It keeps things cold."

Grayson sighed. "It panders to slow drinkers who sip beer like Pharisees."

"Pharisees?" Sarah said, sounding like she was sixteen and reaching for her next assignment sheet.

"The hypocrites," Grayson said. "The ones who say they drink for the taste."

"Fuck the Pharisees," I said, and Sarah snorted.

"The devil's got hold of you tonight," Grayson said.

"If you see him, tell him to fuck off."

Grayson sighed and let his head sink forward so far I was sure a prayer had begun. If I spent another minute near him, I would be calling hell's travel service for a reservation.

Sarah made me follow the clinic physician's suggestion. "This might be a warning sign," she said, repeating that sentence a dozen times in one weekend until I decided it was easier to be strapped to an office full of gizmos that announced death was near than to hear her say those words another time.

The doctor, three days later, watched as his assistant wired me up. The pads on my chest were connected to wires attached to a monitor that, as soon as she turned it on, featured a set of plummeting numbers. It was miraculous, I thought, my brain turning to mush. I'd contracted unconsciousness as a side effect of the swine flu vaccine.

"I'm feeling the exact same way," I mustered, before I slumped over that examination table, waking, seconds later, to the busy fingers of the nurse peeling off the pads. I put my head between my knees without waiting for instruction. When I looked up, the doctor said "Remarkable," leaving it to me to decide if I'd returned from unconsciousness or death.

"I'll run an hour for you on that treadmill," I said. "I'll climb a simulated mountain with a sack of stones on my back. I have the heart and lungs of a teenager as long as you leave the room and take the machinery with you."

"Medicine can't be practiced in the dark of superstition and fear," the doctor said.

"Sure it can," I said. "Doctors have done it for thousands of years."

He frowned in a way that made me certain the wires and pads were coming back like a reoccurrence of hives. "Try concentrating on something you enjoy this time," he said, and when the nurse smiled, I conjured a uniform fetish, the state of her body under all that white. And then, afraid of the measurable consequences of that fantasy, I switched to sports projections. Serving and volleying in my head as the pads approached. Teeing off straight and true and following that drive with a sweet seven iron to six feet from the pin. Laying a multicolored spinning ball right over the spot. By the time I hit an overhead for a winner, ran in the birdie putt, or swung a wide hook into the pocket for a five-bagger, I'd survived the small trauma of that physical exam without additional embarrassment.

I knew the psychology of fulfilling expectations. I was a teacher, after all. And, true to one claim I'd made, at least, I sustained the pulse rate of a hamster so long I could have qualified as an astronaut.

"There's a name for what's been happening to you," the doctor said, "if you care to hear what science has to say."

"Dropsy," I suddenly thought, recalling a name that had the whiff of prophets and faith healers about it. I kept my mouth shut, though I knew I'd have to look up that archaic word before it turned into something I'd contracted. "Sure," I croaked.

"You've been experiencing vasovagal episodes."

Finally, I had a name for it. A routine medical phenomenon, the doctor explained, after his nurse went off to prep another patient, a man who wheezed into the adjoining room with the gait of a student being summoned to the front of the room to give an impromptu speech. I wished him the good cheer of sexual fantasy and then listened to that doctor tell me I wasn't unique. Not even rare. Barely uncommon. I carried home the list of symptoms and read them to Sarah over dinner: "Nausea. Fainting. Orthostatic hypotension. Insulin metabolism. TMJ. Sympathetic and parasympathetic tone."

I laid the jargon-covered paper on the table between us. Sarah forked up three slices of zucchini and held them just above her plate. "See?" she said.

I told Sharon Stegler, the woman who taught business classes in the room across from me, while we waited out the fifteen minutes required of us after the last bell of the day. "Don't tell me," Sharon said. "I have problems like that."

I laughed. "At least now I can tell everyone trying to save me what to expect before I start to go as cold and clammy as something that needs sunshine to induce movement. Next time I'll just read off my pulse and blood pressure numbers from memory until I faint."

"Oh God," Sharon said, "excuse me."

She backed through the door, so pale I expected her to sprawl just short of her desk, pulling a Selectric typewriter or two down with her. By the time I managed to lurch the first steps toward apology, she was sitting in her chair with her head between her knees.

I couldn't even slip away discreetly and hope she didn't know I'd followed her. I said, "This thing is like secondhand smoke."

"Worse," she said. "You feel like you're dying immediately instead of worrying what's coming in another two decades."

Although the inoculations seemed to have killed a few people, the swine flu didn't come to those who refused the shots out of indifference, the fresh fear of malpractice, or faith. Instead, in January, the blizzard of '77 swept into upstate New York like a plague brought by the saint of heavy snow.

Grayson, as we watched from his two-hours-early emptied room the deluge of flakes being whipped by fifty-mile-an-hour gusts, didn't volunteer any names when I asked him about the saints for weather. "The scores on the state tests come out today," he said.

I nodded. The principal had told me the first week of school that the local paper published those scores, that letters to the editor and the school board spread like chicken pox the following week. "We put a lot of stock in those little numbers," he'd said. "By Groundhog Day you'll be wishing for the worst winter of all time if you come in low."

"How low is low?" I'd said.

"If you're perfect like Jim Grayson," the principal had answered, "you don't have to worry about that."

Two weeks after Christmas the principal had made a show of standing just inside my door after school with a stack of tests bound in plastic. "The little beauties are here," he said. "Time to keep score."

He turned as Grayson came through the door. "And here's who the town looks up to," the principal pronounced like a beauty-pageant host. "Seven hundred and thirty-eight passing scores in a row. All that Bible study breeds goodwill with God."

Grayson left with the principal, but a minute later he was back with a set of old state tests in American history. "Your predecessor was just tossing them out like used Kleenex," he said. "Pass them out and use them. There's no answer key, but a teacher doesn't need that to score them. And then work from there to show them the ropes. And keep the test booklets from this year. Start building a file."

He tapped the tests and dropped them on my desk. "Did you know the principal always does his class visits right after the scores come out? The better your student scores, the better evaluation you'll get. I have five years of tests on file. It takes two weeks to get through them all." He looked at me and then at the tests. "What?" he said. "You think I'm not thankful my angel told me to keep those test booklets my first year?"

"Invite him for dinner," Sarah had said that night. "I prefer the crazy to the hard-of-heart."

The blizzard seemed to ratchet up another notch as we watched. I'd put off the invitation, telling myself if I managed a score in the 90s I'd ask him. Those scores were being unwrapped as he stood there, but right then it was impossible to see to the ground from the second story window. I imagined a murder taking place below us, the killer as invisible as one of Grayson's devils. The principal's secretary came on the PA to call all of the teachers to the gym. It looked like a pep rally inside. Like we had a winter Olympics lined up, and a couple of hundred students, by the looks of it, were there to psyche up our school's ski and skate teams. "These are all the bus students whose parents didn't get here before the roads closed down," Sharon Stegler said as the principal motioned for us to huddle around him.

"You have a choice," he said. "Make your own way home or stay here and babysit until the storm blows away."

"When's that supposed to be?" came from several points along the circumference of our miserable circle.

"Not before tomorrow."

I looked at Grayson and Sharon Stegler. "What if everybody leaves?" I asked in a lowered voice, keeping my heresy to a minimum.

"I know the way home," Sharon said, making it sound like a line from a hymn. "He wouldn't give us a choice if he didn't know how few of us live within a mile."

"It's a whiteout for walkers, too."

"There are houses on both sides of the streets. I couldn't get lost if I tried." She glanced around the circle. "What about you—you going for it?" she said to me.

"No."

"You live a block closer than I do."

"I asked my common sense, and it kicked me in the ass for even considering going outside." I looked at Grayson, who lived so close to the school he could pick up his mail between classes, and he gave me the look I imagined seeing if everything he claimed about eternity turned out to be true.

Sharon shrugged and said, "Well, if they find me frozen to death, then I'll get religion as soon as they thaw me out."

I stayed in the gym with the students, and Grayson walked home in the snow, safe as I was unless he slipped and hit his head on the cement stairs leading to his front door. I thought of Sharon Stegler toughing out nearly a mile in this, whether she could imagine herself into a vasovagal episode when the snow took out the landmarks she was counting on, what she would look like sitting in a drift, head between her knees, waiting for the episode to end.

The principal passed around copies of our town's weekly newspaper. "They delivered a dozen just before the storm hit," he said. "The school board always gets personal copies of this issue at their Monday meeting, but there's no way we'll be meeting on Monday." He pressed the copy he was giving me into my palm as if it had a sharpened edge. "Something to think about," he said, and I kept that newspaper folded in my hand like a billy club, telling myself I'd open it when privacy permitted.

After an hour we herded the students into the cafeteria and served them pizzas and milk and ice cream bars. When we returned to the gym, the floor was covered by the two wrestling mats, and I knew we were there until morning. *King Kong*, the original, came on the six televisions somebody had set equal distances apart around the gym. "There won't be a problem with students wandering around to switch from one television to another," the principal said. "They'll see they're stuck."

The students paid attention. They gave themselves up to the ape. It was later, when, with nothing else to do, some of them asked to read the newspaper I'd opened to the test scores before I'd taken a bite of pizza at a table I'd selected because no one was sitting within twenty feet. I'd managed a 91 percent pass; Grayson had 100 percent, another in his twice-a-year run of miracles. I wondered who the saint for test scores was; I wondered if I could ask him.

I leaned back against the bottom row of bleachers, thinking about lights-out, how likely it was that students would slither across the mats during the night, moving back and forth between the boys-only side and the girls-only side. Two of the boys who'd borrowed the newspaper whooped and passed the paper to a third boy who, a moment later, whooped in turn.

"What's up?" I said. I recognized those boys. They were sons of farmers; they took pride in never taking a book home. All three were confirmed failures. "This is us, right?" one said, pointing at the column of scores, and when I didn't disagree, he added, "I hope they don't go back and grade those tests again because I know I left almost half of my answers blank."

"So did I," the boy beside him said. "Maybe the Preacher really does get God on our side."

"See?" I heard from above me, and I looked up at the principal, who was holding out his hand for the newspaper. He was beaming at the three boys, all of whom shrunk back as if they expected to see a paddle materialize in his hand. "One hundred percent. Even you boys can do it if you set your minds to it."

And then the third boy, still holding the newspaper, said, "I didn't even fill in half of mine. Preacher said only answer the ones you know for sure."

The principal looked puzzled. "What?" that boy said. "You think I set my mind to do that bullshit test?"

Looking back, without the blizzard Grayson might have skated through like he'd been doing, apparently, for years. During reasonable weather, those boys had no more chance of talking straight with the principal than they had of going straight home to study. And then there wasn't school for a week, giving the principal time to investigate, reexamine the files, and say something to the superintendent.

By March the superintendent had arranged a hearing. The principal, fueled by embarrassment, had current and former students lined up to testify how unlikely it was they could have passed. Those boys from the gym were reminded there was a corroborating witness to their inadvertent confession.

The school allowed Grayson to use his accumulated sick days until his case was resolved. When she read that the hearing was only a week away, Sarah called him. "You never invited him," she said. "We can listen."

"But not for dinner," I said.

Sarah smiled. "Better than that. We'll be in public."

The following night we were sitting around a pitcher of beer, and Grayson was pouring his into a plastic tumbler, the water he'd ordered sloshed into one of the three frosted, pint-sized mugs the waiter had placed on the table. "I'm trying to save them," he said. "That's what teachers are supposed to do." He pushed the water-filled mug to the very edge of the table, its sides dripping into a widening circle.

"What do you expect the school board to do?" I asked.

"They'll take the Pilate route," Grayson said.

"What?"

"Never mind," Grayson said, but I'd had time to recover. I didn't have to check a Bible to know his reference. I wondered if he would say such a thing in public, splitting the world into saints and devils. He was being offered a chance to resign. He could avoid the hearing where he might offer up the Jesus defense.

"I never changed an answer," Grayson said after we'd all poured a second beer. Those tests were completed with pencils, blacking in the circles labeled *a* through *e* like I'd done on the college boards six years before. "I filled in a few they left blank. There's a difference."

"If they're uncertain, they're told to guess," I said. "There's no penalty for wrong answers."

"Yes, there is," Grayson said. "It proves you don't know. A blank just shows doubt. And I never filled in any more than was necessary to get them to 65 percent."

"How many is that?" Sarah asked. She looked excited, leaning toward Grayson as if he were telling war stories.

He nudged the water-filled mug until part of it hung over the edge. "They're not all like those boys your husband heard in the gym," he said. "There's less than ten of them that need more than five answers." I watched as he slid the mug another fraction of an inch. I was guessing that the next nudge would take it to the floor when Grayson added, "My defense is my motives are not for personal gain."

"You should tell them," Sarah said, her right hand reaching halfway across the table before it settled by the nearly empty pitcher.

Grayson rested his index finger against the mug. "What?" he said.

I thought Sarah was going to put her hand over his, but she kept it on the table, her fingers fluttering slightly before she said, "About wanting to save them."

"People won't see it that way," I said. "They see your name in the paper and they see you as somebody interested in being in first place in the teacher's league."

"I did this long before the paper published such things," Grayson said, but saying what you intended was so weak a plea, it seemed, just then, better not to explain at all, and I ordered another pitcher, the waiter sweeping the extra glass away while Grayson kept the tumbler in his hands. Now that he was ruined, Sarah seemed to want to find reasons to believe in one thing he'd told us, and I had to admit I felt something for Grayson that seemed close to loyalty, and it surprised me. Would I have discovered that feeling if Sharon Stegler had been called on the carpet for using books that had sexually explicit passages or frequent obscenities?

And then I started to form a small measure of sympathy for Grayson because he was being drummed out of the school by men who made their living manipulating numbers—the principal, for one, and the insurance executives, bankers, and salesmen who sat on our school board.

"Playing God can be a good thing," Grayson said. "In movies and books they always make the person out to be an asshole."

Asshole—the word sounded like a blade spinning through the air when Grayson said it, and it cut through my platitudes about the principal and the school board. If Grayson hadn't been caught, I would have hated him as long as he worked in the same hallway. Once a man is broken for things you disapprove of, he becomes someone else, and Grayson, I thought, was now somebody I might like when he was no longer a missionary.

"There's a self-righteousness about it people can't abide," I said.

Grayson nodded. "Still," he said, "those people revere the God they believe in despite him calling the shots in such an arbitrary way."

"You could teach at a parochial school," Sarah said.

"That's not for me. The joy is teaching the ignorant."

Sarah left that hanging in the air between them, but Grayson seemed agitated. "You know what the principal said to me when I told him that? 'Some, Mr. Grayson, might say what you're teaching is ignorance.'" Grayson pressed his hands against the top of the table, leaning so heavily his arms quivered a moment before he stood straight and said, "That's the same person who once sent me a note that read 'Sixty-five is a magic number — the newspaper doesn't item-ize.'"

He stood over us, and for a moment I thought he was capable of lifting the nearly empty pitcher and bringing it down on my head. "The devils are pleased with what we leave undone," he said.

A week later, the day before the hearing, Grayson accepted a paid leave of absence for the rest of the year. The school hired a substitute, waited two weeks, and then began to advertise for a replacement.

Sarah seemed disappointed, as if she had thought she was getting to know a martyr, and now Grayson was just someone who had recanted. By the first week in May, when he was standing in his yard as I passed while walking home from school, his name hadn't been spoken under our roof for nearly a month.

"Look at this," Grayson said, gesturing me onto the brick path that ran toward the north side of his house. "Isn't that something? Here it is the beginning of May, and that snow from January is still here."

I stepped off the walk. The ground was as soggy as if it had rained steadily for two days, but in the shadows behind his house, there was a mound of snow deep enough to cover my shoes. I didn't know about the physics of such things, but I thought maybe Grayson was right, that the last snow to melt was the first to fall, that this gray ice had been here since King Kong fell off the Empire State Building on six screens in the gym.

"It wasn't to impress," Grayson said then.

I stared at that snow while I thought of something to say. "You could have taken Sarah's advice. You could have gone to the hearing and told them the numbers," I tried.

"It's just my word."

I nodded, and then I reached down and clawed up a handful of the ancient snow. It packed so hard in my hands I thought I might be able to kill somebody if I hit him in the head. That afternoon it had to be sixty degrees at four P.M., and the shock of the ice on my hands seemed odd, the way it had when I'd stored snowballs in the freezer when I was ten. I'd forgotten about them until a hot day in July, but when I looked behind the stacks of vegetables and meat, they were gone. My mother had thrown them out. "What would you want with snowballs in the summer?" she had said. "They'd just make a mess."

Squeezing that ice, turning it to something like a snowball while Grayson rambled, I felt dizzy. I'd had one more vasovagal episode since that night Sarah and I had sat with him in the bar in March, going so clammy while a nurse drew blood for a routine exam that she'd gone, without speaking, to a small refrigerator, pulled out a small can of orange juice, and peeled back the tab before handing it to me, saying only, "Drink this."

I hadn't even complained. I hadn't lowered my head, still standing over an imaginary putt even as I foresaw death and the answer to Grayson's research projects. "You'll feel better in no time," she added then.

"I don't feel sick," I said. "I feel wrong."

"Projections are good," she said. "What activities do you most enjoy?" And then she'd tossed the tab into the wastebasket and begun to print on the label wrapped around the vial of my blood.

I stepped back on the bricks, looked for something at which to throw that packed ice so I wouldn't have to hold it any longer. "There's no good way to excuse what looks like cheating to everybody but yourself," I heard Grayson saying. "I know that for a fact." He bent down and packed a snowball of his own, but just then he sounded as if he'd been preparing those words like a press release, and I pushed one foot backwards and then the other, working my way toward turning back up the street.

And yet I saw that Grayson understood that once you do such a thing, apologies don't work, that explanations don't work, that people, in the face of learning about how things have been assigned to them, can't tolerate an explanation. They want to be able to say, "That's just the way it is," and let it go at that.

I worried that snowball in my hand, watching Grayson's expression. He looked as if he was searching his library of demons and angels for exactly the right example of someone torn to pieces because he didn't know when to shut up. "Saint Cassian," I blurted, "the one who gets stabbed to death with pens by his students."

Instead of acknowledging my story, Grayson looked perplexed. I'd expected the recognition that promoted camaraderie, something I could imagine reflected the small success of my good intentions.

"Who told you that?" he finally said. "Who's passing along that old story as if it were true?"

"It isn't?" I said.

"The students had to stab him," Grayson said. "He'd been sentenced to death."

I fired my snowball then, pivoting and thunking it into the thick trunk of the willow tree in the yard across the street, but Grayson kept his in his hand, something, I thought a minute later as I started back up the sidewalk, he'd done to avoid shaking my hand.

I had the rest of the walk home to remember the afternoon I'd seen the individual copies of my state tests and confirmed that out of 140 students, 13 had failed. Three of those thirteen had missed by one point, three more by less than five points. The other seven, as if they had spent the first four months of school on Mars, had missed by ten points or more. I'd stared at those three near misses for a long time, weighing the difference between 91 percent and 93 percent and wondering how many answers I could fill in before the proctor arrived to collect the tests. And then, including the next three students, I imagined the difference between 91 and 95, going into the files, finally, to find the results from the year before. Eighty-four percent had passed the preceding January; 86 percent had passed the June test that was approaching, and I'd thought 91 percent good enough, figuring myself for an improvement over Mr. Drake, the man who'd quit, not been fired, who'd had tenure with those scores as if the school accepted that 15 percent of its students were damned.

The Armstrong View

"It's a miracle," Reynolds's wife said, and surely his children believed it because all three of them, each old enough to be living away from home, looked awestruck. Their father had undergone brain surgery. His skull had been opened and closed again after a part of his brain had been removed.

Not a large part, the surgeon had explained, just a blood vessel or two, a bit of cerebral cortex, and the hemorrhage that had threatened his life had been controlled, Reynolds discovered, without him turning into a drooler or a limper or one of those people who slurred their speech and stared vacantly at family members they could not remember. And indeed, he wouldn't tell any of them, he'd expected the worst, yet here he was recovering so perfectly he was reconsidering his position on miracles.

"What do you want for dinner to celebrate?" his wife said.

"Let's go to the store together, Lauren," Reynolds said. "Let's impulse buy before all this giddiness wears off."

"OK," she said, but as soon as they walked into the store, Reynolds realized he meant only meat, and Lauren waved him on, saying she'd pick up a few things while they were there.

Ten minutes later Reynolds was carrying four pounds of strip steaks for his family, glancing down six aisles before he found her among the pet food. "There's only the three of us," Lauren said. "The boys can't help you with that on their way back to Maryland." She smiled like the happy puppies and contented cats on the bags and boxes, and then she glanced at the ceiling.

"They've ruined another 70s hit," she said. Reynolds listened to a song that seemed as unfamiliar as the ones he never recognized in his college fine arts course when the instructor had placed the needle in the middle of a movement and challenged the class to identify as many musical elements as it could.

"Really?" he said.

"Come on, Greg," she said. "'Stayin' Alive.'"

"That's 'Stayin' Alive'?"

"Sure. The tune's still there. It's just turned to mush by all those strings."

"I'm lost."

"You're so literal these days. Fifty years old, Greg, fifty-one in less than a week—this should be the beginning of the figurative era."

"The Hope Metaphors. If they were so valuable they'd be under glass."

Reynolds lifted a carton of milk bones from the shelf. The dog on the package looked as if it were listening to the next song. His wife said "See, another one ruined."

"I'm sorry," Reynolds said, "I don't know that one either."

"Stuck in the middle with you," she murmured to the recorded tune. "Here I am, stuck in the middle with you," bobbing her head as if she were wearing earphones.

He looked back at the happy dog on the box and concentrated on the sounds from the ceiling speaker. "I'm still lost," he finally said.

"What'd they do, take out your memory of pop songs?"

"No, I remember the song. 'Clowns to the left of me, jokers to the right,' Jesus, we have the record somewhere, but that doesn't sound like Stealers Wheel. It doesn't sound the same at all."

"Of course not. It's muzak."

At dinner, while they finished the strip steaks, Reynolds's daughter told a story: "They had auditions at the Upstairs today," Sarah said. "The second biggest theater in the city, and this woman who went first belts out the song they were using—you know the one, the potato, potahto song."

"'Let's Call the Whole Thing Off,'" Reynolds said.

"Sure," Sarah said.

"The Gershwin brothers."

"Exactly, only she sings it, 'You like potato, I like potato; you like tomato, I like tomato.' No difference at all."

Reynolds laughed. "The literalist," he said. "Didn't she notice the rest of the song? Maybe she's been selling shoes longer than you have."

"But you don't recognize the songs you own," Lauren said, frowning. "A literalist is a middle-aged man who won't admit he knows a song because it's not the version he owns."

"Oh, it's no big deal," Sarah said. "I've been immune to Dad's shoe store joke for six months. There's a guy at work who has a real problem."

Reynolds waited. He looked at his wife and repeated "'Potato, potato; tomato, tomato,'" three times before Sarah began.

"His baby died of SIDS. He found it not breathing, and then, when the ambulance got there, they didn't have any oxygen in their canisters so they couldn't revive it."

"It probably didn't matter," Reynolds said.

"That's not the point. It means the baby had no chance."

"Zero times zero."

"He's suing," Sarah said.

"That's what autopsies are for."

The next day, driving south on his first postrecovery solo car trip, it looked to Reynolds as if two men were working flag, and because they were smiling he was certain they'd chosen to stop the line with his car as the result of some kind of bet they'd made.

Suddenly, it was more than he could bear. He wanted to drive head-on into the oncoming line, but instead he opened the door and approached the men.

"Might as well stretch some," the man with the flag said. "Soon as we get that there line through we're blasting."

Reynolds checked the expression of the second man for signs of a smile, but he simply said, "Back to work. Them rocks'll soon be waiting."

"Hell of a job," the flagman said to Reynolds. "Ged does hand work on the rocks they don't get with the lifter."

"Chain gang," Reynolds said at once, and the flagman nodded.

"Damn betcha," he said.

The last of the cars rolled by, and horns sounded along the line behind Reynolds's car, but the flagman shut them up by posting his STOP/BLASTING sign.

"This is really something," he said to Reynolds. "You know you can see this from the moon?"

Despite himself, Reynolds looked up at the cliff side to evaluate. No way, he said to himself, but he decided to wait for the flagman's explanation.

"Armstrong saw the Great Wall of China from the moon. You can see the Great Wall, you can see this—it's a hell of a lot bigger."

Reynolds remembered the photographs taken from space he'd seen of the earth. No feature like the Great Wall could possibly be seen. "Is that right?" he said, and then a puff of dust rose from the cliff and the roar reached them a second later.

"Yessir," the flagman said. Boulders tumbled down the hillside and thundered onto the wide swath of leveled land. Reynolds followed the dust cloud that drifted across the highway toward the river, which, according to the flagman, must also be detected from the moon.

"They say they followed a dragon's path when they built the wall," Reynolds said. "That's why it doesn't go straight."

"Bullshit," the flagman said at once.

"They say they planned so well they only had one brick left when they finished."

"Tell that one to the boss," the flagman said.

"I don't think it was Armstrong said he saw the Great Wall. I think it was one of the other astronauts."

"You're the expert, looks like. This line'll be moving before you know it, and you can study up some at the library."

Reynolds shrugged. "Check on it," he said, walking back to his car and thinking, suddenly, about something he knew was true. Two weeks before, while he was still in the hospital, an Amish buggy carrying seven children had lurched in front of a truck on a section of the road already completed, the horse spooked somehow by the difference the new road made, the speed, and the truck had broadsided the buggy, catapulting the children, ages four to seventeen, onto two lanes and the shoulder. Miraculously, only two of them had died, one other permanently maimed, the horse put down on the spot. You'd have to be closer than the moon to see the consequences, Reynolds thought now, but he'd read all four days of the newspaper's accounts at once, and while everyone, during the first three days, had anguished over the children, suspecting the truck driver had been drunk, Reynolds's first thought had been the foolishness of the family putting seven brothers and sisters into a buggy, the driver a child herself, and sending them along a four-lane highway.

"It's because you're reading the story all at once," Lauren had said, "that you feel that way."

Four hours after he watched the cliff explode, when Sarah stopped by to visit after her shift at the mall, Reynolds started right in, "'Eether, eyether; neether, nyether,'" he said, but Sarah didn't smile.

"The guy at work has changed his story. He says he fell asleep on the couch with the baby and then just rolled over on it while he was sleeping."

"He actually said that?" Reynolds asked.

"People at work believe him. You should see how fat he is. If he just moved at all he'd smother something."

"I don't," Lauren said. "That's impossible, what he says."

"My story's worse, too," Reynolds said. "It seems I can remember all the words to songs, but I don't recognize much of anything if I just hear the tune."

"It'll come back, Dad. You're just blocking."

"Your mother watched me work at it just before you got here. I never knew a song until somebody sang."

"Oh Dad, there's a million people who can't do that."

"But I wasn't one of them until the operation."

"You're the luckiest man in the world is what you should be thinking, Dad."

"I know."

"And?"

"It doesn't help."

"You keep things like that to yourself or else everybody will hate you."

"He's not going to broadcast it, Sarah," Lauren said. "He knows it's just music he may have lost. All he has to do is think of the other choices."

"I think about them all the time," Reynolds said. "Which one is next to go."

"So you would be missing two things then," Lauren said, but Reynolds could tell she was thinking ahead, anticipating.

"Assuming I had everything to begin with."

"Why not?"

Which was where Reynolds knew this should stop because a list suddenly scrolled down as if it had been called up by software. Which files could not be reopened?

He hated himself for even thinking of a computer. They were terrible inventions, he was certain. They lost things entirely, pages and pages of material vanished. But worse, they remembered so much and didn't care at all about any of it.

After midnight Reynolds went downstairs in his underwear. He carried a pair of sweat socks to pull onto his feet so they wouldn't cramp in the chill, and then he tucked the earphones on his head and turned on a tape he'd made years ago of his favorite instrumentals.

"'Wild Weekend,'" Reynolds said to himself at once, but then he spun the tape in fast forward so he wouldn't remember a title because of the order of the songs. He walked to the picture window while the old tape squealed and hissed. Outside, the yucca plants had covered everything near the house and closed up so thickly the windows couldn't be opened.

He was supposed to chop them out because, according to Lauren, "Pretty soon we'll have nothing but yucca plants. It'll look like a damp spot in the desert instead of a yard."

When he saw somebody walking on the road behind the yard, Reynolds stopped the tape and watched. It couldn't be a woman, he thought, not alone at nearly 1 A.M. And whoever it was was probably concentrating on the space around him, not dawdling to search dark windows for the sight of a man in his underwear.

Reynolds reached behind him and pressed *play*, and when he turned back the figure was gone, disappeared more quickly than he would have thought. While he listened to the unrecognizable saxophone solo, he watched the end of the forsythia row to see if the man would reappear.

What had attracted him to this song nearly forty years ago? The saxophone player was dreadful, the tune simple, and suddenly Reynolds was certain the man outside was standing behind the forsythia and peering at him through the branches.

When the next song began, another saxophone, another repetitious hook, Reynolds pulled off the headphones, laid them aside, and took off his underwear so he stood naked except for the sweat socks and the headphones he put back on. They might as well have been earmuffs for all he was hearing.

He knew the song was "Poor Boy," "Bust Out," or "Flamingo Express" because the tape was near the end. They were the last three songs. He remembered their order exactly from seven years ago when he'd recorded them from his 45s. His genitals shriveled in the cold, and he shivered. Nothing about his naked body would arouse anyone, not even a full-time voyeur.

When the song ended, the tape stopped. "'Flamingo Express,'" he said to himself. That was the last tune he'd squeezed onto the forty-five-minute side. Reynolds turned to shut it off, laid the headphones down, and when he walked back to the window he thought the man might be standing in the yard, but there was nothing outside but the pale haze where the moon tried to break through the clouds.

Two days later, because he knew his daughter wasn't working, Reynolds entered the shoe store and dawdled near a display of loafers until the fat man she'd described approached. "Can I help you?" the man said.

"Maybe." Reynolds pointed to three different styles. "Size 11," he said. "I'd like to try them on." He turned and read the name tag to be sure it said "Justin Mickley."

"Be with you in a jiffy."

"Take your time, Justin," Reynolds said, and he sat with one foot on the inclined plane of the salesman's stool. He wanted the full treatment, and when the fat man returned, breathing heavily, he was glad the 11s had been either high or low in the store room.

His shirt had ridden up, and a flap hung over his belt. When Justin Mickley's tie shifted to the side, the tugged buttons showed a fold of flab.

Reynolds feigned interest. He walked around the store in the right shoe of all three pairs, each time walking behind the salesman, pleased that Mickley turned as if he were afraid to have somebody walk behind him.

"Remember those shoes that came to a point in the front. Those were the days," Reynolds said.

"Can't say I do."

"There was a name for that style—the hoods wore them so I bought a pair and thought I was one step closer to being a criminal."

"Before my time, I guess," Mickley said.

"A shoe salesman ought to know the names for something like that. History's important. I was a disc jockey once, and I knew the names for everything from rock and roll's past."

"That one you have on is called a loafer," Mickley said. "The first one is called an oxford."

"How about the other one?" Reynolds said.

"I don't know."

"A balmoral," Reynolds said. "That's the old-fashioned name for those hood shoes." Justin Mickley started to slip the loafer off Reynolds's foot, keeping his head down. "Those pointy-toed shoes hurt like hell if you did any walking in them. I think they were made just for slouching. You know, looking cool and sullen with those pointy toes showing attitude where somebody could trip over them. They were weapons, but they rubbed me raw."

"I never heard of a balmoral," Mickley said. "You want attitude, I have these shitkickers."

"No, to tell you the truth, I don't want any of these shoes. I think I'll just live with the ones I have."

"You're the boss."

As Mickley retied his old shoes, Reynolds saw Sarah walk in. Payday, he thought. She's here to pick up her check.

He gave her the choice of speaking to him or not, and she glared over Mickley's shoulder and kept walking to the sales counter without saying a word. A song on the overhead speaker caught Reynolds's attention. He listened while Mickley reboxed the shoes, and then he asked, "What's the name of that tune?"

Mickley looked puzzled, but he said, "'Hey, Jude'" before he added, "I thought you were a disc jockey who knew his stuff."

"That was before I forgot everything. That was before I had to start relearning the way things are."

A new song began. "What's that one?" Reynolds said.

"'Yesterday,'" Mickley said. "Listen, I'm through with you, mister. I need to do some useful work."

"The shoes that are round in front are called bluchers," Reynolds said. "The old names are being forgotten."

"You sit here and listen to the Beatles, mister," Justin Mickley said. "You do whatever you want." Sarah was watching from the cash register. She was holding her check as if it were a receipt for something defective she wanted to return, and she didn't try to catch up with him when he left the store and window-shopped for a few minutes to give her that chance even though, the afternoon before, Lauren had made an appointment with a doctor, and he had twenty minutes before he was supposed to be tested.

Before they started, the doctor joked about the tests he was about to administer. "This is painless," he said. "So simple we give it to dogs to see which ones will try to sing along."

"I'll try to keep my mouth shut," Reynolds said.

When the first tune began Reynolds thought it was a control test to measure if he were lying on the easy tunes which would follow. The melody was so foreign nobody would know it except the grand champion of *Name That Tune.* He thought of reclusive monks, forbidding climates, a culture tucked away from mass media, and then he shook his head slowly and said "No idea."

The doctor nodded and cued his CD to another number. The song sounded like a vanity telephone ring, something silly jangling through a twelve-room house while the guests giggled and cooed approval. "No idea," he said again.

The doctor frowned after the fourth tune, and then his lips parted quickly as if he'd caught himself. "The forest and the trees," he said. "These are right in front of you, Mr. Reynolds."

"Nevertheless," Reynolds said, "I don't recognize any of them."

"Let's try one more," the doctor said, and Reynolds sat up this time and said, "That's really catchy. If I'd heard that one before I'm sure I'd know it."

The doctor switched off the CD player and leaned back. "Do you want to know what you've been listening to?"

"Sure," Reynolds said. "It's not like I'm waiting for CAT-scan results."

The doctor didn't smile the way Reynolds expected. "'Jingle Bells,'" he said. "'Three Blind Mice.' 'Row, Row, Row, Your Boat.' 'America.' 'Silent Night.'"

"Whatever it is, I've got it bad," Reynolds said.

"Amusia," the doctor said. "Rare, but not unique. Listen for a moment or two to these."

Reynolds identified chickens, turkeys, a chainsaw, a jackhammer, and a dog as soon as the doctor shut off the tape and asked. He named all five songs he'd heard before the doctor had read him one line of lyrics from each. "See?" the doctor said, and indeed, Reynolds saw.

"It's the end of pleasure," he said.

"Not at all," the doctor said. "You can enjoy nearly everything."

"That's what they say when you check in at the retirement village before you start the three stages toward death."

"Mr. Reynolds, we're not talking about anything but a tiny bit of brain here. You're years from the retirement village."

Instead of driving straight home, Reynolds took the back roads until he was five miles south of the Amish buggy-crash site. He passed a dozen Amish farms along the way, driving below the speed limit as if the men behind the horses would judge him more favorably. Not once did he see a child.

When he turned left at the highway, he began to accelerate, reached 65, and kept it there. Three trucks passed him before he reached the crash site, a fourth was alongside him when he saw the skid marks, and he realized that except for the news story, he would be doing faster than 65 on this section of new highway where the police winked at speeders until they passed 75. Anyone who permitted unsupervised children near here was as guilty of murder as a man who rolled over on a baby, Reynolds thought, and then he lifted his foot from the gas and allowed the car to slow until he heard a blare of horns so close he braced himself against the steering wheel.

He felt like a passenger, that whatever happened to the car was in the hands of someone chewing gum and turning up the radio against the onslaught of sleep. He would be better off to open the window and let the wind fill his eyes with grit. He needed some discomfort to keep him going. And when no one hit him, he pulled onto the shoulder and tried to imagine himself opening the door and stepping out without looking.

"Surprise," Lauren said, when he walked in. Sarah stood behind her, sticking candles into a cake. "The boys can't be here anyway, and since Sarah works tomorrow night, I thought we'd celebrate your birthday the day before."

"I have amusia," Reynolds said. "Did you ever hear of it before?"

"The doctor said that's what he would test for."

"He told you that?"

"Yes, when I called him yesterday."

"Ahead of time, he'd guess like that?"

The three of them sat down to chicken wings and Lauren's disclaimer of "It's only once a year."

"What did you think, Dad, you had a tumor?" Sarah said. "You just had your brain on display; somebody would have noticed. And what was all that about being a disc jockey? You were never on the radio."

"I could be one now. Everything I played would sound new."

"Just the instrumentals, Greg," Lauren said. "You're making more of this than you need to. And everything else, for that matter—Sarah told me about you grilling that salesman."

"Enough already," Sarah said. "Dad's the birthday boy. He has to finish two dozen extra spicy to show he's still as good as new."

Reynolds wiped sauce from his chin and dove into a second helping. "Fifty-one," he said. "I'd eat them if you made that many."

"Go ahead, then," Lauren said. "You're going back to work on Monday. You just walk in and do it."

"Unless they ease me to the side a bit."

"You don't have to audition."

"Yes, I do," Reynolds said. As if on cue, both his wife and his daughter pushed their plates slightly forward to signal they'd had enough of trying to eat the food he loved.

"Well, this'll cheer you up, Dad," Sarah said. "It turns out the police are saying now that Justin smothered the baby on purpose. They say he did it for the insurance he and his girlfriend took out on the baby when it was born."

"Who takes insurance out on a baby?" Lauren said.

"Exactly."

"So why was he showing your father shoes today?"

"He's out on bail."

"And?"

"He's still working because they're afraid to fire him because he might be innocent."

Lauren sucked in her breath, but Reynolds gobbled another wing and looked so placid his daughter said, "Dad, don't you think all of this is terrible?"

"Of course," Reynolds said, and then he emptied the rest of the platter onto his grease-soaked plate.

"I don't think you do. I think you're just saying that because you can't say otherwise and be human."

"That's a mouthful," Reynolds said, smiling, and his daughter looked horrified.

"Oh my God," she said, slowly and unlike herself, and Reynolds fought back the urge to say, "What's wrong?"

"I think everybody's capable of terrible things. Why would anyone believe otherwise?"

"I'm not," his wife said.

"Sure you are."

"What's wrong with you?" Sarah said.

"Nothing," Reynolds answered, which seemed the truth.

"I think it would be better to be wrong than to be like you. I know what you were doing with Justin today."

And Reynolds wanted to tell her she was right, that he wished himself evil, but there wasn't any syntax for his confession, and without a way to arrange itself, the confession disappeared like a once-heard, but never-recorded melody.

"Well, come on, you're fifty-one now, and you've showed you can eat as many chicken wings as either of your sons," Lauren said, adding five hours to his age, and she carried the birthday cake to the table on a dish he'd never seen before. She reached under the platter and turned a small handle and a tune began.

"Is this another song I liked once?" Reynolds asked. "Is this a present for the man who knows no tunes?"

His wife and his daughter watched the cake go around, the candles flickering in the small drift of air. When they didn't speak, he knew it was "Happy Birthday" he was hearing.

Reynolds lifted the cake down, blew out the candles in three puffs, and started to slice it before the empty dish stopped turning. "Here," he said, but they waited for him to take the first bite before they lifted their forks. The cake tasted like ash. He thought Lauren had left out some ingredient and was waiting to see if he had noticed.

Gatsby, Tender, Paradise

At quarter to eight, Saturday morning, Russ Bridgeford's daughter enters the kitchen dressed and carrying her car keys. "This is special," Bridgeford says.

Lauren nods and opens the door. "See you later," she warbles, and then, without a syllable or gesture of sarcasm, she's gone.

"Does she have detention?" Bridgeford asks his wife.

"She has other places she can go on Saturday mornings," Kim says. "One of them is having her English teacher invite her to breakfast."

Bridgeford lets the newspaper droop. "And that's OK?" he says.

"It's Perkins at 8 A.M., not dinner at his house."

She sounds so defensive Bridgeford is relieved. Perhaps he hasn't missed some change in acceptable behavior. "Anyway," Kim goes on, "Beth's going with them."

"He invited both of them?"

"Apparently," Kim says, and everything in her tone tells him she's labored not to accuse herself of needless fear.

"You worry about the wrong things," Lauren says when she returns. "There were two of us. We just ate and left."

Bridgeford has mowed the lawn, washed a car, taken a shower, and shaved. "And that took two hours?" he asks.

"We smoked cigarettes and drank coffee for a while. We talked about things."

"Things?"

"Whatever. You know."

Bridgeford, beginning with *ménage à trois,* considers some of the things he would list under the heading of "Whatever," and all of them have the common denominator of sex. "And that's it?"

"So far."

He feels himself turn dark inside. "So far?"

"He said 'I hope we can do this again sometime.'"

"Why you two?"

"He's been doing this for years, Dad. He's harmless. Everybody knows who the real perverts are. Mr. Martone wouldn't bother buying me breakfast."

"The biology teacher? The Mafia wannabe?"

"There's plenty of stories."

"Stories?"

"You know."

"But he's not your teacher. He doesn't even know you."

"I see him at track, but don't worry. All he does is give me the creeps. He's so obvious Grandma would know what he's after."

On Sunday, Bridgeford walks the Gettysburg battlefields with Harry Austin, who's driven them nearly two hours to examine bullet holes in cabins, pockmarks in rocks. "Imagine yourself striding with Pickett's men across this field," Harry says, "how long it would take to reach Cemetery Ridge, how much of that walk would be within range."

"I think I'd run," Bridgeford says, though already his arthritic knees ache from the irregular surfaces, from the ups and downs of exploring Civil War sites.

"Let's just walk it," Harry says. "Let's find out for ourselves what a half mile of open land makes us want to do."

And then, looking at the ridge where Harry's pointing, Bridgeford stumbles in a chuckhole, feels his knees begin to scream. "Christ," he mutters, shaking his head and testing himself through ten cautious steps.

He starts an apology, but Harry waves it off and strides toward the ridge. Bridgeford slides to the side and drifts toward a nearby cabin. Somewhere up ahead, according to Harry, is Little Round Top, but he sits in the cabin's shadow and watches Harry walk. He can tell Harry's watching the hillside in front of him, that he's guessing when the bullets would start reaching him. If he walked like that, Bridgeford thinks, he'd tumble altogether, break a leg maybe, and save himself from real and imaginary slaughter.

A small group of tourists appear and pass him without speaking. There are three of them, two women and a man, and they seem, to Bridgeford, to be disoriented. One of the women walks oddly. Multiple sclerosis, he guesses, the last months before she gives in to the cane. The other woman listens to the man as if he were a tour guide. She cocks her head, follows his gestures.

Later, at the souvenir shop, he sees those tourists again. They're bunched with twenty others, and the woman who walked oddly is being photographed. "What's up with them?" Bridgeford asks.

"Another scam," Harry suggests. "Maybe that guy takes pictures at the battlefield like they do at the mall with Santa Claus."

Bridgeford nods and searches behind the woman for the sort of background someone might pay for. He sees nothing but postcards and sweatshirts and sets of miniature soldiers dressed in blue and gray.

The following Saturday he discovers the woman's photo on the first page of the second section of the *Patriot*. It turns out she was part of a convention of lightning strike and electrocution victims, the survivors ferried by chartered bus to tour Gettysburg because they'd gathered just thirty miles away in Harrisburg for three days of bonding into support groups.

The woman in the photograph had been struck by lightning out of a blue sky. She'd been water-skiing and was revived by a man who had learned CPR the week before. "I feel blessed," she told the reporter, "but then again I don't." She suffers from memory loss, motor function problems. She can't water-ski, even if she had the courage to try it on another cloudless day.

Bridgeford finishes the article. Another woman had been zapped during acupuncture. A chef had been numbed permanently by a short circuit in his mixing bowl. And one man claimed to be disabled from a light-switch shock, something Bridgeford has survived several times. If the Confederates had outlasted bullets as luckily as these people had survived overdoses of electricity, he thinks, they might have marched right up the Susquehanna River to where his great-grandfather was playing with hoops and wooden horses.

Lauren shuffles past. She looks like her teenage Saturday self again, and he's relieved she's not dressed. "I said *no* this time."

Bridgeford smiles. "I don't have a poker face," he says. "What excuse did you give?"

"I didn't give an excuse, Dad. I said I didn't want to go with him, period."

"Good," he says, though the word seems like a lie.

"He'll get somebody else. It doesn't matter."

On Friday, Lauren gets a paper back from the English teacher — a C+ instead of the A- she received on the one before. Bridgeford thinks both of the papers are C work, but he reevaluates the acquiescence of the girls.

Bridgeford watches his daughter eat breakfast and follows her body. He sees there is one more button she could fasten on her blouse, that her skirt seems unfashionably short. When she leaves, Kim slides into her chair. "You don't want to judge from a breakfast menu," she says. "People don't often do what they think about doing."

Bridgeford shakes his head and listens for Lauren's car backing out of the driveway. "He wants to have it happen to him," he says, "not make it happen. He wants to avoid guilt."

"You can't think like that and have a happy day."

"Yes," Bridgeford says. "Exactly."

He drives to Perkins the next morning at 8 A.M., takes a table in the smoking section, and orders. Just after the pancakes arrive, the teacher walks in with two girls Bridgeford doesn't know. As soon as the waitress brings their menus, all three light cigarettes.

Bridgeford, it turns out, is facing the girls. They laugh softly together, neither of them beautiful. He begins to feel as if he's judged badly.

The teacher, the first time Bridgeford makes out what he's saying, is giving the girls a sort of memory quiz. *"Tender is the Night,"* he says. *"The Great Gatsby. This Side of Paradise."* The girls repeat the titles, but Bridgeford is paying attention now, trying to get all of what the English teacher is saying. "OK," the teacher says, "we'll get back to that when the order comes."

"You want us to remember?"

"I want you to say *The Waste Land, The Love Song of J. Alfred Prufrock, Four Quartets*."

The girls chant the titles with the enthusiasm of small children, and then their breakfasts arrive. "OK," the teacher says, "do the Fitz-gerald."

"*The Great Gatsby*," they offer at once, but then they pause. "*Tender is the Night*," one of them says, and then they're both stuck.

"That was only a minute," the teacher says.

"It's too much like a test," one of the girls says. "We get nervous."

"Try the Eliot."

"*Prufrock. The Waste Land*," they both say, and then, after a few seconds, "*Four Quartets*."

"See?" he says. "See how easy? Try these: *Junkie. The Naked Lunch. The Soft Machine*."

The girls laugh. "You're making those up," one says.

"Burroughs," the teacher says, "but all of his boys are gay."

A minute later, Bridgeford hears the girls repeat "*Junkie. The Naked Lunch. The Soft Machine*."

That afternoon he asks his daughter, "Did you play that game?"

"*Gatsby. Tender. Paradise*," she says at once. "I got an A."

"Did you do Burroughs?"

"The junkie gay guy?"

"Anybody else like that?"

"You mean sexy? We did Anaïs Nin."

"*The Delta of Venus*."

"Sure, but I never heard of her."

"What were the other two titles?"

"I have no idea."

The next Friday Harry tells Bridgeford he's been secretly building a car for five months. "I've finished enough for it to look like something," Harry says, while he opens the barn. "A Morris," he says, and though Bridgeford has never heard of it, the name sounds British, like something James Bond would drive on his days off.

"How much of the car came to you in one piece?" he asks.

"The engine, mostly, and the drive train. The rest is from a dozen old Morrises. People place ads in a magazine I subscribe to. I answer them, and we agree on terms."

For over forty years Bridgeford has excluded himself from this sort of correspondence. The other side of the garage, he notices, is stacked with auto parts. "Extras," Harry says, "and disappointments. I'm learning here. They'll make a good start on the next one."

Bridgeford nods as if this news is ordinary. In his garage, where he used to park his car, are stacks of magazines and newspapers, bags of folded cardboard, containers of bottles and cans. The last Saturday of each month he has to drive this debris to a loading dock where Boy Scouts unload it for recycling. He imagines those boys rooting through a Saturday's worth of magazines, finding pictures of naked women and matching them to the fathers of girls they know at the middle school.

The beer Harry produces is in green, seven-ounce bottles. Before Bridgeford swallows, he knows it will be warm. "The British way," Harry's told him, though it seems to Bridgeford to be as much a misjudgment as spending half a year in an auto-body shop.

"I just leave it on the back porch. Nobody bothers it. It doesn't take electricity," Harry reminds him while Bridgeford decides the car looks quaint, something that would turn heads until it broke down and left you stranded among mechanics who had no compatible parts or ideas about where to get them.

By the time Harry brings second bottles, a girl Lauren's age runs toward them along a path mown through the field that stretches behind Harry's farmhouse. Susan, he remembers, and he watches her run with the assurance of the trained and conditioned.

"Isn't that something," Harry says, so spontaneously Bridgeford easily nods. "Two runners for daughters," he adds, "and I struggle to walk a couple of miles through battle sites. She runs with Elaine some mornings, and I marvel."

Bridgeford knows Harry's older girl won the district championship a few years ago, had gone off to college but was back home and working at the bicycle shop near the mall.

Before Bridgeford leaves, Harry gives him three weeping beech trees to plant. "I have fifteen acres," Harry says. "They won't be missed."

The weeping beech are a struggle to unload. Bridgeford is astonished the root balls weigh so much, that Harry had lifted them so readily. "Hernia time," Lauren says, getting out of her car as if she's waited for the third one to settle beside the driveway.

"Good timing," he says.

"I was listening to the news."

"So how's Humbert Humbert these days?" he asks.

"He's getting married again," Lauren says.

"Really?"

"It's not one of my friends, Dad. He didn't get one of us pregnant." He waits for her to go on, but she seems disinterested, goes to the newspaper box, pulls the afternoon edition out and scans the front page.

"But his wife is young?"

"Twenty-two," Lauren says, not looking up.

"A former student?"

"Yes."

"Breakfast at Perkins."

"Jesus, Dad." She walks past him, crosses the porch.

"All those eggs and cigarettes. He'd better enjoy her while he can."

"You don't know that," she says, slapping the paper against her palm.

"You buy enough breakfasts, you get something in return." She walks back and shoves the newspaper at his face. A picture of Martone, the biology teacher, is on the front page. He's wearing a dress shirt two sizes too small. If he weren't wearing a tie, Bridgeford thinks, you'd be able to see his chest where the buttons pulled apart. *Teacher Arraigned*, the caption reads.

"The cops took him right out of class," Lauren says. "They could have waited."

Bridgeford reads a paragraph about sex with students, about two of them bringing charges. "They don't owe him any favors," he offers.

"They wait ten years. They could wait another half hour."

Bridgeford, in the next twenty-four hours, learns the vita of Frank Martone, the disgraced teacher and track coach. He taught biology, tenth graders who were likely to go to college. He recruited distance runners from each class. The skinny girls, the ones who wanted to be skinny, something he guaranteed if they kept to his training schedule.

He showed them pictures of former star runners, and they were pleased to be chosen. The school had a succession of district champions, and some of them placed at states.

Above all, the girls saw how thin and toned the old runners were, how they could enjoy eating and stay desirable. And Martone following their bodies as they ran was nothing the boys didn't do. They could say *No* when he asked them to stay after school; they could refuse the rides he offered after practice, and no, he'd never forced any of them, they said, all denial except for the two seniors who had filed the charges.

"We had sex in his classroom," one said. "All he did was lock the door and turn out the lights."

Bridgeford thinks of how Lauren's body looks with her arms thrown up in happiness at the end of a race, how her shirt, sweat-soaked, sticks tightly to her breasts. He imagines the English teacher scouting for breakfast guests. Which parts of Lauren excite a man who shows those girls pictures of himself from fifteen years before, his long hair and leather pants, his guitar posed suggestively at the hip in the pictures of the band that had released one self-made album.

That track coach ran with the girls. He put himself behind the best of them, reminding them about form and pace. He had miles to memorize the ones he wanted.

"Once in a blue moon," Kim reminds him, reverting to her mother's expression.

Bridgeford stares at her. He tells her there are years when there's no full moon at all in February, that this year was one of them, and it would come back again in less than thirty years, something like the necessity of the military draft.

"You're making too much of this," Kim says. "Your daughter is safe, and now the rest of the girls will be safe."

"There's no end of assholes."

"I read that article about February," she says. "The last time there were blue moons in January and March but no full moon in February was 1866. The next time that happens will be two and a half million years from now."

He goes outside and chooses spots for his three trees according to where the grass is worst, and within a few minutes, discovers why. Stones and clay. The first two are bad digs, but he tells himself this will be worth it, three weed-infested, nearly bare spots gone, three trees added.

The third is the worst. He discovers a piece of asphalt which fits into the soil like a built-in shelf. He wedges it up, yanks, wedges and yanks again, and it tears back into the clay, lifting the earth over a foot away.

His house was built after the neighbor's, and he imagines the contractor tossing debris into the vacant lot. Finally, it heaves up and out, half as large as a card-table top. He decides not to lift it, flips it over and over until he reaches the crown vetch that smothers the hillside. In a couple of weeks, he thinks, this will be covered.

A minute later, retrieving the shovel, he thinks the third tree is planted so close to the house its roots will work at the foundation in a few years, that the house itself seems to be staring at his foolishness. And when he steps toward the back wall, he sees two side-by-side indentations, both of them so deep there are hairline cracks running from their edges through the siding.

Rocks, he decides at once, examining the ground at the base of the wall, and then the shrubbery, surprised at finding nothing. Whoever threw the stones would have had to be extraordinarily accurate from a distance or have stood so close, he would automatically retrieve them.

"The prick," Harry says an hour later, the two of them evaluating the arrangement of his trees. "And him all these years in the naval reserve, the goddamned prick."

"It's a tough one to live down," Bridgeford says.

"I'd take a dollar for every teacher who's screwed a student, and then I could stick to cars and history instead of squeezing the spare time out of my life at work."

Bridgeford thinks it's a wager Harry wouldn't lose. "Betting on behavior is too easy," he says.

"That's what war's about," Harry says. "Looking out over acres of open land and figuring the odds of men facing up to a human wave."

"That's disappeared now."

"Not hardly," Harry says. "Martone took to his heels. And him wearing his uniform in every yearbook my daughters have brought home. That's why we have dress codes—school's not a Halloween party."

Bridgeford knows he disagrees, but he's willing to wait for Harry to wind down. Moral outrage seems suddenly the single correct choice on the SATs of decency. To bring an absolute to current events. To say NO.

"Enough of that," Harry finally says. "He's off to jail, and your trees aren't going to attack your foundation. The only thing you have to worry about is who would bother slamming golf balls into your siding. And such a good shot at that."

In the morning, every local newscast leads with the story of how, an hour after he was released on bail, Frank Martone walked into the woods behind his house and shot himself through the roof of his mouth. Bridgeford tries to guess how many seductions would drive somebody to suicide. He keeps his total to himself, and until they are finished eating their late Sunday breakfast, nobody else in his family says a word about Frank Martone.

"Let's get this over with," Lauren finally says.

"We don't know anything," Bridgeford starts.

"Of course we do," Kim says. "A molester every day among all those girls."

"Get real, Dad," Lauren adds, and Bridgeford looks from his daughter to his wife, decides to hold back anything he might say about complicity and blame.

"Such a coward," Kim says. "To think—such a scum and then a coward twice over."

"What happened to the blue moon theory?"

"He was alive then," Kim says. "He was an example."

Before he fishes the newspaper from the box the following Friday, Bridgeford waters the new trees, checks their leaves as if he expects to find them swarming with beetles and aphids. All three seem as healthy as nursery stock.

On the table, when he sets down coffee and the newspaper, he sees Lauren's homework spread beside a short stack of books. It's an essay on "The Worn Path," and Bridgeford fixes on a few lines in the opening paragraph. "The night before my grandmother went to the hospital for the last time, she had me bring her the dictionary so she could fill in the four blank spaces in the Sunday crossword puzzle. 'You finish what you start,' she said to me."

Bridgeford reads all of it, the best essay Lauren has ever written. He tells himself to ask about her grade when the paper is returned.

The newspaper, when he opens it, carries a letter to the editor by Harry's daughter Elaine. The letter recounts how the dead teacher had comforted her in his car when she was upset about her performance in a cross-country race.

"It was more than my running," she wrote. "I was sixteen. I was miserable about a hundred things, and when he hugged me I felt happy. And then he kissed me and said, 'Doesn't that feel nice,' and it did, in a way, and then he opened my blouse and told me how beautiful I was, that I should be happy to have such wonderful breasts, that they were a gift, and then he raped me."

Bridgeford is puzzled by the description. It doesn't sound at all like rape, and yet thinking about the teacher who took his daughter to breakfast makes him want to take a cue stick to the teacher's head.

Harry's daughter, he knows, is twenty-four years old. The teacher, according to her, had been raping students for several years before she met him. "Everybody knew," she wrote. "I knew."

And then Bridgeford thinks of Harry holding a warm beer on his porch, watching his daughters across a hundred yards of open field striding in together from the miles of their morning run, both of them trained by the dead teacher. Harry will be holding the newspaper like a letter from the army's condolence office, and, Bridgeford hopes, he will begin to speak instead of crawling under that Morris with a handful of tools.

Acknowledgments

The stories in this collection first appeared in the following journals.

"The Lightning Tongues"	*South Dakota Review*
"Sorry I Worried You"	*South Dakota Review*
"Cargo"	*Arkansas Review*
"The History of Staying Awake"	*Cimarron Review*
"Piecework"	*Beloit Fiction Journal*
"The Serial Plagiarist"	*Other Voices*
"Wire's Wire, until It's a Body"	*Sonora Review*
"Rip His Head Off"	*Seattle Review*
"Book Owner"	*Santa Monica Review*
"Pharisees"	*Cimarron Review*
"The Armstrong View"	*Mid-American Review*
"Gatsby, Tender, Paradise"	*Cimarron Review*

The Flannery O'Connor Award for Short Fiction

David Walton, *Evening Out*
Leigh Allison Wilson, *From the Bottom Up*
Sandra Thompson, *Close-Ups*
Susan Neville, *The Invention of Flight*
Mary Hood, *How Far She Went*
François Camoin, *Why Men Are Afraid of Women*
Molly Giles, *Rough Translations*
Daniel Curley, *Living with Snakes*
Peter Meinke, *The Piano Tuner*
Tony Ardizzone, *The Evening News*
Salvatore La Puma, *The Boys of Bensonhurst*
Melissa Pritchard, *Spirit Seizures*
Philip F. Deaver, *Silent Retreats*
Gail Galloway Adams, *The Purchase of Order*
Carole L. Glickfeld, *Useful Gifts*
Antonya Nelson, *The Expendables*
Nancy Zafris, *The People I Know*
Debra Monroe, *The Source of Trouble*
Robert H. Abel, *Ghost Traps*
T. M. McNally, *Low Flying Aircraft*
Alfred DePew, *The Melancholy of Departure*
Dennis Hathaway, *The Consequences of Desire*
Rita Ciresi, *Mother Rocket*
Dianne Nelson, *A Brief History of Male Nudes in America*
Christopher McIlroy, *All My Relations*
Alyce Miller, *The Nature of Longing*
Carol Lee Lorenzo, *Nervous Dancer*
C. M. Mayo, *Sky over El Nido*
Wendy Brenner, *Large Animals in Everyday Life*

Paul Rawlins, *No Lie Like Love*

Harvey Grossinger, *The Quarry*

Ha Jin, *Under the Red Flag*

Andy Plattner, *Winter Money*

Frank Soos, *Unified Field Theory*

Mary Clyde, *Survival Rates*

Hester Kaplan, *The Edge of Marriage*

Darrell Spencer, *CAUTION Men in Trees*

Robert Anderson, *Ice Age*

Bill Roorbach, *Big Bend*

Dana Johnson, *Break Any Woman Down*

Gina Ochsner, *The Necessary Grace to Fall*

Kellie Wells, *Compression Scars*

Eric Shade, *Eyesores*

Catherine Brady, *Curled in the Bed of Love*

Ed Allen, *Ate It Anyway*

Gary Fincke, *Sorry I Worried You*

Barbara Sutton, *The Send-Away Girl*